HABOOB WIND

Tommy Anderson

Published by
Coyote Mountain Publishing
CoyoteMountainPublishing.com

Cover & Interior Book Design by Monkey C Media
MonkeyCMedia.com

Copyedited by Adrienne Moch
Author Photo: William Kidston Photography

Printed in the United States of America

ISBN: 978-1-5136-3423-4

Library of Congress Control Number: 2018940312

"Freedom is never more than one generation away from extinction."
—Ronald Reagan, 40th president of U.S. (1981 - 1989)

For American Patriots

Past,
Present,
&
Future

PROLOGUE

*The term haboob, which refers to a violent Arabic
dust storm, is first known to be used in 1897.*

As technology has made historical leaps in the late 20th and early
21st centuries, mankind, in many facets, has become increasingly
dependent upon the newest and latest technological advances.
From entertainment to finance, the world and almost everyone in
it has become dependent on technology. What was unimaginable
only 25 years ago, and science fiction in the 1950s is now reality.
People from the major metropolitan centers of the world to the
most remote outposts of this planet can converse with one another
in real time, follow current events, keep up with the latest in
entertainment, and monitor their financial status from anywhere.

In the palm of any individual's hand is now a device more powerful
than the computers that took man to and from the moon in
1969. The young and old alike have lost themselves in artificial
worlds and many have become oblivious to current events. Social
evenings in bars that had centered around the topics of local and
even international events have now been replaced with selfies and
the latest app craze for the smartphone.

The world has become so dependent on multiple smart applications and semi-artificial intelligence programs that it would come to a halt as we know it if something would ever happen to interrupt this flow of data, even for a short time.

The panic that took place on the evening of December 31, 1999 would be nothing in comparison to the loss of these systems via a massive outage. We are now a world dependent on satellite systems, the Internet, electronic banking, and electronic and voice communications. Some have projected a return to a virtual stone age existence in the event of a massive disruption to these modern tools of civilization.

The governments of the world have taken note of this, but they have not yet fully addressed those sounding a warning to provide the protections needed to respond to the full ramifications of such a scenario. However, many people around the world are very aware of this vulnerability and are preparing to exploit it to advance their reign of dominance and terror.

In the event of a situation of this magnitude—which would cripple an entire nation or nations—there will stand a few brave heroes who will emerge to rescue us from what will become known as "The Haboob Wind."

THE EXODUS

In the early morning hours of December 11, 2011, the air was crisp and cold from the overnight chill of the Iraqi Desert. The sunrise was a brilliant array of blended colors—purple, red, and orange—against a cloudless blue sky. The entire scene anywhere else would give a sense of peace and solitude, but in this location, was anything but that. The morning stillness was occasionally broken by several barking dogs and the low voices of groups of men discussing the events that were unfolding that day.

At roughly 0545 hrs., Captain James Hansen from Hampton Roads, Virginia looked at his olive drab patrol watch. Eight months before, Deputy Sheriff James Hansen was working patrol in rural Virginia, southwest of Washington, D.C., when he was notified that his Virginia Army National Guard Unit—C Company 116th Infantry Brigade Combat Team (Stonewall Brigade)—was being called to active duty in Iraq. This unit's lineage, as reflected by its name, stretched back to the American Civil War and the early days of the Virginia Militia. In fact, several members of the unit, including the Executive Officer, First Lieutenant Willis Schneider of Manassas, Virginia, descended from Civil War veterans. Lieutenant Schneider shared the name of his great-great grandfather, Willis B Schneider, a Major with the 10th Virginia Infantry who was killed at Gettysburg nearly 150 years earlier while serving as a Brigade Commander during General Picket's infamous charge on Cemetery Ridge.

This would be Hansen and his National Guard Unit's second tour of active duty in three years, with the first being a deployment to Afghanistan in 2008. Now, he was serving as Company Commander in the 3rd Brigade, 1st Cavalry Division. Hansen and his men, who he called "My Ginny Boys," would provide point security and reconnaissance protection for the U.S. military's exodus from 11 years of involvement in the War Against Terror and Saddam Hussein in Iraq. His 10 armored Humvees would be the tip of the spear if any trouble erupted on the long road back home. Captain Hansen and his command staff knew the eyes of the world would be on this movement and their actions this day. Unbeknownst to Captain Hansen and his superiors—ranging all the way to the White House—other eyes were watching this withdrawal intently as well.

Looking again at his watch, it now read 0558 hrs. Instinctively, Captain Hansen turned to his Executive Officer and said, "Lieutenant, have the boys fire up and get ready!"

Lieutenant Schneider replied, "Yes sir, Jimmy!"

Captain Hansen then gave a small smile and slowly shook his head back and forth, thinking to himself, "Willis, how many times have I told you not to call me Jimmy in front of the men?" He then turned to his interpreter, who had become his friend during this deployment. They had often exchanged stories about life back in the States and the future of Iraq after American forces left. "Sheda, I will miss you my friend, and if possible, maybe in the future we will see each other again," Captain Hansen said while firmly shaking his interpreter's hand.

"We shall see what the future will bring us, James, but until we see each other again, may Allah keep you safe," the interpreter replied, then slowly walked away from the convoy.

Looking down the line at the men standing next to their Humvees, some silent, some chatting, some laughing, Hansen thought to himself, "I'm going to miss seeing these boys every day when we get home." He then knelt and scooped some Iraqi sand into a small baby food jar, thinking that he wanted to put it on his desk back home as a remembrance of these days and his men. He never wanted to forget them, and he knew his men felt the same for the most part. They were not just an Army combat team—they were also friends and family who had been through some remarkable experiences together. These feelings were not unique to this Army National Guard Unit—they ran deep within all reserve units. Whether you were a Commander or a Private in the command structure, the men you served with were also your neighbors, coworkers, friends, and even family back home.

In the early morning of December 11, 2011, Lieutenant Schneider picked up the microphone in his Humvee and made the broadcast they and all America had been waiting to hear for 11 years: "Spear Leader to Spear Two, over."

The radio crackled back with the voice of Sergeant First Class William Jennings of Richmond, Virginia: "Spear Two, go ahead, over."

"Spear Two, fire them up top. Have our boys keep their eyes open this morning, over," Lieutenant Schneider replied. The morning stillness was then broken by the increased sound of men's voices and the roll of multiple engines being started. Dust was being kicked up along the highway as more dogs started barking and several birds flew away from the adjacent buildings. Captain Hansen looked at his watch again and reached for his radio handset. With it now being 0600 hrs., he was now about to make history in his command Humvee and told his Ginny Boys to head out toward Kuwait.

One after another, the 10 armored Humvees from Stonewall Brigade began to move, heading down Highway 80 from Baghdad City on their nearly 300-mile trip toward Kuwait.

The procession of Humvees was not even 10 miles out of Baghdad when two U.S. Army Apache attack helicopters flew over them at about 1,000 feet, providing air reconnaissance and support should they need it. As they moved down the infamous Highway 80, Captain Hansen thought to himself how ironic that they were on the famed "Highway of Death" from the first Gulf War in which the Coalition air forces lead by the U.S. had nearly annihilated the Iraqi Army in 1991. He then silently whispered a prayer, "On this day Lord, please don't let history repeat itself!" Now, Captain Hansen and his men had more than those two Apache attack helicopters watching their back. Several USAF and CIA drones were also flying surveillance of the exit route from as far as 25 miles on either side of the highway. In addition, U.S. Department of Defense satellites had also turned their sights on this nearly 300-mile strip of highway.

After the convoy had traveled approximately 100 miles on the road back to Kuwait, one of the lead scout trucks had a mechanical problem and the convoy had to stop. While mechanics looked at the Humvee, a perimeter scout reported a reflection in the desert that could have been several clicks to their left. Captain Hansen took note of the report and radioed it to his brigade headquarters. The Apaches had headed back to their base to refuel and their replacements had not yet arrived to take over their convoy-covering duties.

Brigade headquarters advised they would see if the Air Force could send some aircraft to check out the sighting. The Air Force scrambled two F-15 Eagle fighters that were on patrol nearly 100 miles away. The two fighters were from the 144th Fighter Wing of the California Air National Guard in Fresno, California. Lieutenant Colonel Billy "Gutter" Adams radioed to his wingman Major Steve "Rocket" Randall: "Rocket, I hope this is simple stuff, over."

"Roger that, Gutter, we are too short for this," Major Randall answered with a chuckle.

"Roger that, I've got 20-plus in and my papers are going in when we get back to California. This Air Force is changing too much for me, brother," Lieutenant Colonel Adams replied.

"Rocket, we are about 20 out. Let's drop down for a look, but all I see right now is desert and the convoy," Lieutenant Colonel Adams radioed.

"Gutter, I got the target at 2 o'clock. It looks like the reflection is off the windshield of a wrecked truck," Major Randall advised.

"Roger that Rocket, I will come in behind you and confirm," Lieutenant Colonel Adams reported, then added, "Affirmative, a wrecked truck appears to be no threat."

With that, Lieutenant Colonel Adams reported back on the status of the report and advised they would remain in the area to support the convoy until the Apaches returned. Shortly after Captain Hansen received the report of no threat in the area, Lieutenant Schneider requested a radio and status report from all the other Humvees. In turn, each Humvee reported there was no contact with insurgents or in fact anything suspicious at all outside of the reflection. Captain Hansen was then informed that the mechanical problem had been taken care of and the convoy could continue. As he looked at his map, he thought to himself, "Maybe this will really be a good day," the convoy continued its exodus from Iraq.

While America's military and intelligence forces were focused on this exodus, it had created the prefect distraction 100 miles away in Mosul, where insurgent forces were preparing to hold their first official meeting to plan their long-projected war against America. As the U.S. Army convoy began to move again and continued its way toward Kuwait, a man in desert camouflage emerged from under the wrecked truck and used his cell phone to contact some of the many other hidden eyes watching the convoys leaving Iraq that day. This would continue throughout the day; as the vehicles passed predesignated points along the highway, reports would continue to flow out from burner cell phones. Each message, which was sent by text, was immediately destroyed to prevent tracing. The status reports funneled back to the insurgency headquarters, to an Al-Qaeda brigade commander with the code name "Scorpion." This news was assurance his day would be clear for the historic meeting with representatives of the various radical Islamic groups to formulate their plan for moving forward after the American military exit from Iraq. The various insurgent factions, despite their differences, agreed to start working together toward a final solution to the "Great Devil" America.

THE SWIRLING
WINDS

The ink hadn't even dried on the signatures attached to the Status of Force agreement signed during the term of President George W. Bush and the Republic of Iraq when the initial planning stage of Haboob Wind began to be formulated. Through numerous negotiations with the new Iraqi government, the Bush administration had sought an agreement to remove the U.S. military in stages from Iraq after the removal of Iraqi dictator Saddam Hussein and the stabilization of the insurgent threat. As a result, in 2008, the U.S. Iraq Status of Forces Agreement was signed, effectively ending the American military involvement within the Iraqi nation. What it managed to do was to pass the situation onto the next U.S. president, in the hope that an equitable arrangement would be hammered out to provide security to the region and protect American interests in the area. The Status of Forces Agreement included a deadline of December 31, 2011, by which, "all of the United States forces shall withdraw from all Iraqi territory."

Closely following the progression from the date the agreement was signed until the moment American military units were exiting

Iraq was an unassuming Iraqi named Seem Abu Sheda, who had assisted the U.S. military as an interpreter until their exit from Baghdad. Unbeknownst to the Americans, Sheda was a rising leader and brigade commander within Al Qaeda and the Iraqi insurgency. Sheda was quite astute on life in the West, being born and raised in an Islamic neighborhood in London, England. After he acquired an undergraduate degree in business at Oxford, Sheda went on obtain his master of political science at UC Berkeley in the U.S. Being a model student, Sheda also worked in several community centers in the Berkeley area and was quite friendly and popular among other his other classmates. Because of this, Sheda managed to stay under the radar of the U.S. Department of Homeland Security and even had clearance to volunteer on several political campaigns involving local Democratic candidates as an intern while doing his master's dissertation. Upon returning to his home in the UK, he advised his parents he would be relocating to Iraq and wanted to help the new Iraqi government establish itself after the fall of Saddam Hussein.

Shortly after his arrival in Baghdad, Sheda was assigned to assist the U.S. forces in rebuilding neighborhood infrastructure that had been neglected or destroyed under Hussein's reign. In fact, he even began to work directly alongside the American Army as an interpreter and was considered by many as a friend. Sheda was not considered a threat by the U.S. and as a result was exactly where he had planned to be—well under their suspicion.

Sheda's position as a commander in Al Qaeda had gone undetected and he managed to remain an unknown to both the coalition and Iraqi intelligence sources. In fact, Sheda was so instrumental in the hierarchy that he was slated to become a general in a new insurgency that had been growing in the shadows, awaiting the withdrawal of the American military from the country.

This new army, called the Islamic State of Iraq and Syria, would be soon known by the acronym ISIS and would eventually strike fear within Iraq and throughout the world. ISIS would go on to seek revenge and retaliation against those within the Islamic states who aided and assisted the West in the invasion of their country.

This target would also grow to encompass those who would not strictly adhere to their warped version of Islam. In time, this movement that was initially considered around the world as a minor disenchanted group of terrorists would grow to become the most feared terrorist group and abuser of human rights since the Axis forces during World War II. This feeling of fear would be shared by every country on the globe.

The news of the pullout was now being reported on the Iraqi state radio as Sheda was driven through the northeastern portion of Baghdad, away from where he had said goodbye to the convoy commander, Captain James Hansen. Faintly smiling, he looked over a territorial map highlighting U.S. and coalition forces locations and felt the vibration of a disposable cell phone that was in his breast pocket. Taking it out, Sheda saw a two-digit code that indicated the American convoy was now headed out of Baghdad and other locations around the country. Knowing the American forces were on the departure route out of Iraq, Sheda turned to the driver of his Mercedes Benz sedan and sighed, "Finally. Take me to the café." The driver glanced into the rearview mirror and his eyes connected with Sheda's; he gave a slight nod, and then looking forward, took the next right turn down a dusty, abandoned alley on the northeast side of Baghdad. The "café" was the code name of a predetermined location in Mosul for the gathering of a few select militia leaders under Sheda's command, the place they had planned to meet when the exodus from Iraq had been initiated. What began to unfold on that day was the planning for the retaliation against America that would take place on America's home soil and go right up to the entrance of the White House.

Reaching into his right pants pocket, Sheda pulled out a small disposable Bic lighter. He then took the SIM card out of the disposable cell and ignited it in a small dish that was next to him in the back seat. After the SIM card had finished burning, Sheda rolled down the rear window of the car and flung the destroyed card out into the barren desert. He then removed the battery from the phone and tossed it as well. Finally, taking a pair of pliers out of the old satchel sitting next to him, he proceeded to destroy the disposable cell phone. Once again, that piece of discarded equipment would find its way out onto the Iraqi desert.

Twenty minutes later, as the vehicle headed northeast of Baghdad, Sheda reached back into the same old cracked brown leather satchel. Shuffling through it for several minutes, he found what he was looking for, a small portable wireless Play Station video game system. Activating it, he glanced out into the clear, blue, cloud-free sky while the game ran through its startup sequence as if looking for a distant American surveillance drone. Sheda then logged into the system and entered a multi-player word game. After staring at the game screen for a few seconds, a notification was received from another player requesting a game challenge. Sheda accepted the challenge and then entered a word to put into play. Known only to a select few individuals, that word was an obscure identifier to the other player that Sheda was, in fact, the individual he had been waiting to hear from. This communications system had been developed years earlier by Al Qaeda technicians as a means for the various cells to communicate with very little chance of detection. After Sheda confirmed the other player's identity through his choice of game words, he entered his coded message. To a casual observer or to the prying eyes of the CIA and Iraqi Intelligence, it would appear only as the normal banter between two game players. The other player was Major Aju Titus, a brigade commander who reported to Sheda as his second in command of the intelligence unit for the newly formed ISIS unit. With a few more moves in the game, he advised Major Titus the meeting was on and scheduled for three hours from then at the café. After Sheda received the coded confirmation of his message, he completed several moves that abruptly ended the game with his loss. Sheda then left the game site and powered off the Play Station. The message was then relayed to other members of this special council in the same manner, sent through their command ranks like dominos falling in a line, until all council members were notified of the meeting. After shutting off the game and making sure the satellite Internet connection was terminated, Sheda placed the Play Station back in the leather satchel, closed the flap and then fastened the buckle to it. Sheda leaned his head back into the rear seat headrest and closed his eyes. He would attempt to get a little rest on the way to the café because tonight would be a late night.

Sheda was jolted awake as the Mercedes dipped into a hole in the roadway left years ago by U.S. air attacks. Looking around through the car windows while shaking himself awake, he saw the outskirts of Mosul. Sheda once again reached for his portable Play Station to let his contact know he was in Mosul and would be at the café shortly. The café was not a café at all, but an innocuous looking tea shop. Getting out of his Mercedes, Sheda spoke to his driver, saying he would be there overnight and to come back tomorrow afternoon. He instructed him to leave the area and stay in his apartment all evening as to not draw any suspicion in case the CIA still was operating drones over Iraq.

Sheda went into the tea shop and looked at several types of tea offered for sale. He then silently slipped behind a curtain into a hallway at the back of the store. Opening a door to the basement, Sheda went down the stairs using a small flashlight for illumination. Once in the basement, Sheda reached under the shelf that contained some of the inventory for the store upstairs, grasping a handle and giving it a pull. In pulling the handle, the entire shelving unit moved forward, exposing a hidden door behind it and a lit hallway. Sheda entered the hallway and pulled the door supporting the shelving unit closed behind him. In the hallway, a uniformed insurgent soldier holding an AK-47 snapped to attention as Sheda nodded to him and walked into the room he was guarding. That very room had at one time been a secret military planning room for the Republican Guard that was used in the first Gulf War.

Long hidden away, the room was truly a secret and perfect for today's insurgent operations. It certainly looked the part of a military operations center, complete with maps on the walls; staffed computer terminals; a large lighted table with a map of Iraq, Syria, Iran, and Kuwait; and finally an array of flat screen televisions that were broadcasting numerous 24-hour news channels along with security cameras covering multiple areas around the café. A broad smile came across Sheda's face when he saw General Mohamad Sedaka. The general had a similar smile as they approached and gave each other a firm handshake along with a firm pat on both shoulders. "Sheda, welcome," said the general. "The day that we have long awaited is now upon us! Come sit down. Have some tea and we shall discuss your plan of Haboob Wind."

Sheda remained standing while the others took their seats awaiting his presentation. Sheda had prepared a multilayered operational plan that would lead to an actual invasion of the continental U.S.

on the 20th anniversary of the September 11 attack on America. Sheda began, "Haboob Wind will result in a final death blow to the Great Satan and put an end to the true infidels threatening Islam and Allah!"

Sheda continued, "The multidimensional plan involves us making several alliances with other enemies of America. Though not our friends, we need to adopt them, at least temporarily, in the name of Allah. The enemy of our enemy will be our friend, at least until our objectives are met. Let me show you how we will accomplish this." With that, Sheda pressed a button on the remote and his PowerPoint presentation illuminated the wall, reading as follows:

1.   We will create a coalition with the Supreme Leader in Iran and have them continue their nuclear program as a facade. We will assist them in developing an "Electronic Pulse Weapon" or EPW capable of disabling all communications, computers, electricity, satellites, and other sophisticated military equipment within the U.S.

2.   A delivery system for these weapons will come from North Korea, which has been developing its ICBM capabilities with the hope of one day being able to rival China with a global reach. To date, its test launches have been failures. This is not true; North Korea is having its missiles fail purposely to give the appearance of incompetence. This is part of our plan of deception.

3.   America and other Western countries will be approached to accept large groups of refugees. We will embed trained Islamic warriors into the refugees they accept. The immigration system in America as in Europe is so lax they will be able to disappear into the country and

relocate in numerous sanctuary cities with very little risk of their discovery. Warriors will coordinate into small teams in the hours prior to the EPW attack. These warriors are sleepers who have already infiltrated their predetermined targets consisting of America's military and first responders.

4.   In addition, we have had our warriors assimilate into the American landscape. As you know, we have been doing this since America attacked us in 1991. Many have now moved into positions of power within the American government, law enforcement agencies, and the American military itself, and some are now in positions of authority. They will be called to action and will assume their true role as soldiers of Islam shortly before the attack commences. They will assist in neutralizing resistance to our invasion.

5.   We have also reached an agreement with some members of the Mexican government; Mexican cartel leaders; and most importantly, members of a group in America called the Reconquist. This group within America and Mexico supports the separation of California, Arizona, New Mexico, and Texas from the U.S., with that land being returned to Mexico. A promise was made to these groups for their assistance in this attack. They will help obtain military equipment and weapons from the Mexican military and assist with specific targets within the southern border.

6.   All strategic goals must be made with the first five to seven days. Any later than that, the success rate will diminish because the U.S. military will start overcoming the equipment failures from the EPW detonation. It is imperative that the designated military instillations be over taken with in this five- to seven-day period. Their

sophisticated aviation equipment and computer-controlled systems will still be neutralized, but their conventional resources will be back in operation.

Sheda then explained how the social climate in America would aid their plan. "There has been an uproar in America over the mass shootings and the use of semi-automatic weapons that were involved in the attacks. We will have our sleepers awaken and conduct sporadic mass casualty attacks across America. Over time, this will weaken the American public's resolve. The voice of anti-firearm politicians will be so strong and the American government's refusal to identify such attacks as terror will aid us. There will be a growing call to ban firearms and even the ownership of specific weapons by the public and the American news media. As a result, by the date of our attack on September 11, 2021, the private ownership of firearms by the average American citizen will be greatly reduced. This will weigh heavily in our favor. We have selected warriors already in place who, when given the command, will create terror and willingly sacrifice themselves, using firearms. This will create a panic, convincing the American leadership to remove weapons from the public."

Silence overtook the operations room at the café when Sheda finished his explanation of the plan "Haboob Wind." No one said a word, not General Sedaka or his command staff. The room was so silent that Sheda began to worry. General Sedaka slowly rose from his chair, then started laughing and clapping wildly. Soon, all the other officers were on their feet clapping and General Sedaka cheered, "Perfect, Sheda. Just perfect!"

NEW
BEGINNINGS

It was New Year's Eve 2012 in Temecula, California and the Beer Garden on Main Street was the place to be. It was hopping with a live band and drinks were flowing. A popular hangout for the military from the numerous bases in the area, as well as motorcycle clubs, veterans, police and firefighters, this was a hot spot. At a table in back sat three friends and their wives. As the band played, they were discussing a business venture they had wanted to go into. They knew what they wanted to do, and tonight was the night to talk about the future.

At the table were Bill "Gutter" Adams his wife Linda, Fred "Redeye" Hoffman with his wife Debbie, and Steve "Stevo" McIntire, who had brought along a date. All three had retired from the military after basically being forced out with the reduction of forces under the current administration. With the wind down of the war, those in power had decided to reduce the military to pre-WWII levels because it was believed America would never again be involved in the type of military conflict that would require a large amount of military personnel or equipment. This had been a common error made by those in power in Washington;

after every major conflict, there was a need felt for a drawdown in personnel. However, every time this had been the case, America was caught off guard and paid dearly for the error with a large loss of American lives and casualties. This time was no different and the feeling now was that small specialty units such as the SEALS, Green Berets, and Army Rangers could do the job. With reliance on drones, satellite surveillance, and highly sophisticated military aircraft that used the highest state-of-the-art electronics and computer systems, a large military would no longer be needed. These friends fell victim to this logic.

"Billy," a former F-16 fighter pilot with the CA Air National Guard, was a victim of the military drawdown in 2011. Even as a decorated pilot with 21 years of service that included Operation Enduring Freedom and Iraqi Freedom, the drawdown left him without a position with the realignment of Air National Guard units throughout the U.S.

Freddie was a victim of the same drawdown when his slot as an F-18 pilot out of Miramar MCAS was eliminated. Freddie was also an experienced fighter pilot from Desert Storm flying the USMC Harrier and in Iraqi Freedom flying the F-18 Super Hornet. Freddie was given the opportunity to move to Cherry Point MCAS, NC and convert to an Osprey pilot. But with 28 years in the Corps and still a young family living in Temecula, he decided to retire. A big factor in his decision was that going from supersonic to VTOL did not excite him at all. Freddie's call sign was "Redeye," which also came out of flight training. He had a slight learning disability and would stay up sometimes all night to keep up with the rigors of training requirements to become a Marine Corps aviator.

Rounding out the trio of friends was Steve, who was in the Marine Corps both on active duty and in the reserve for a combined 28 years when a back injury forced him into retirement. "Stevo" had been a crew chief on several Marine Corps helicopters in his career involving tours in Desert Storm, Somalia, Iraqi Freedom and Enduring Freedom in Afghanistan. He was known as a hard driving, hard partying and no-nonsense Irish-American airman. His talents included being an ace aviation mechanic; if it flew, he could maintain it, fix it or reproduce it.

Tonight's discussion among themselves and their significant others was their plan for the future. Since their lives had revolved around aviation, specifically military aviation, they had come up with a plan that would satisfy that love of plus give them a career. The three had come up with an idea for a new aviation museum in a part of the country where there was no shortage of them. As a result of their love of flying, Billy, Freddie, and Stevo wanted to start the Riverside County Warbird Museum located at the French Valley Airport in Temecula. They were a small group with big plans in an area of the country with an abundance of historic aviation museums.

The three airmen had managed to locate a vintage and partially restored North American B-25 Mitchell medium bomber that was put in an estate sale. Their strategy session revolved around raising the funds to put down on the vintage bomber, then raising more from investors. In October 2011, they officially founded the Riverside County Historic Aviation Museum. located at the French Valley Airport in Temecula.

The only thing missing from the museum was the plane, but together they could get that taken care of. So tonight, they established a plan and a timetable.

They hoped to obtain the aircraft by the end of February 2012 and start their restoration. If it worked out as planned, it would be airworthy and doing air shows by early in 2021. In the meantime, they would look for parts, do odd aviation jobs for extra funds and even create parts unavailable in their machine shop in their hanger. The future was starting to look very bright for these three airmen.

◇ ◇ ◇

In July 2016, FBI Special Agent James Hansen was sitting in the outer office of Assistant FBI Director Rita Johansen at FBI headquarters in Washington. After thumbing through several magazines, he reflected on his journey to this moment in time— being a deputy sheriff in Virginia before the war, being called to active duty with the National Guard and being accepted into the FBI academy shortly after his return to Virginia in late 2012. Since he came home from the Middle East, Hansen continued to fight terrorism, except now through the FBI. Sitting alone in the room, he nervously looked at the receptionist, smiled and said, "How are you today?"

Not even looking up at him, she responded flatly. "Fine."

Hansen thought, "Great Jim, what did you do this time?" In the past, he'd had several run-ins with supervisors over policy and procedure issues, so he figured it finally came to a head. Looking again his watch and shifting himself nervously in his seat, the phone at the receptionist's desk rang. "Yes, Director!" the receptionist answered and then looked up at Hansen saying, "Agent Hansen, the Director would like you to go into her office."

Walking into Director Johansen's office, Hansen encountered his first smile as the Director said, "James, it is so good to see you. Please take a seat." With that, he sat at the one chair in front of her desk, adjacent to two other assistant directors who were seated with manila file folders in front of them.

"James, I'm sure you a curious why we wanted to talk to you today," Director Johansen said.

"Yes, Director, and first I want to apologize if I offended any of my supervisors with…" Hansen was cut off by Director Johansen before he could finish.

"That isn't why you are here," Director Johansen replied. "Actually, in part it is, because we like the initiative you have taken in questioning some of our policies in counterterrorism investigation."

"Really?" Hansen said with a small smile on his face.

One of the other assistant directors stood up and handed Hansen several file folders, which he just glanced at quickly and looked back up. "Agent Hansen," Director Johansen said, "we want to offer you a promotion of sorts."

"Promotion?" Hansen repeated.

"Yes, we are promoting you to supervisory agent and want you to head up a new team we want formed to investigate and help stop future terrorist activity with in the United States," Director Johansen told him. "You will be working directly under my office and will answer to me. We have given you several file folders of people we believe would be beneficial to your team, but pay particular attention to Agent Grafton's and Agent Hamilton's files. They both have unique talents in anti-terrorism investigation and are military veterans."

"Yes, Director, of course," Hansen answered while looking at the folders.

"You will see why we believe they will be assets to your team," Director Johansen said. "Agent Hamilton is an expert in explosives and evidence collection. Note that after high school she enlisted in the U.S. Army as a Military Police Officer. During her time with the Military Police, she went to explosive ordinance disposal training and eventually received a commission as a Warrant Officer 2 assigned to the U.S. Army's Criminal Investigation Division (CID), and from there was assigned to criminal investigations at the Department of Defense in Washington. After six years in the Army, Agent Hamilton applied for the FBI and we hired her in the summer of 2010. Since then, she has worked as a field agent and in counterterrorism intelligence.

"As for Agent Grafton," she continued, "she started her law enforcement career with the Brown County Sheriff's Department in Wisconsin after leaving the Army as a military explosive ordinance disposal technician. In 2011, she applied to the FBI after getting her B.S. in criminal justice from the University of Wisconsin. She also spent several years as a field agent and as an FBI Bomb Disposal Technician. Two years ago, she was transferred to anti-terrorism intelligence.

"We believe they will be assets to your team," Director Johansen stated, looking back and forth at the other directors for their agreement.

"Yes Director. Where will we be working out of?" Hansen asked.

"We are making arrangements for you and your new team here and we should have that arranged before the end of the week," Director Johansen answered.

One of the other directors spoke up and asked, "James, we see you are not married. What about relationships?"

Hansen replied, "I'm quite single with only a few ex-girlfriends. Why is that relevant?"

"Because Jim," Director Johansen replied, "at least initially this will be time- consuming. We are not dictating your personal life, but one of the things we like about you is that you are focused."

"Understood, Director," Hansen replied.

"Jim, we here believe all these lone wolf attacks are centrally orchestrated, and we need you and your team to figure out how and why, then prove it so we can fight it," the Director said.

"Of course," Hansen replied. "I had better get started organizing my team."

With that and a few handshakes, Agent James Hansen now a supervisory
agent, again in charge of an anti-terrorism unit—just this time with the FBI.

◇ ◇ ◇

It was July 20, 2018 and at MetLife Stadium in East Rutherford, New Jersey, a semi-trailer trailer was delivering 10 refrigeration units for the concession stands prior to the start of the 2018 NFL season. Bruce Kanaan, assistant maintenance supervisor, signed for the delivery and directed the installers where to set up the new units. While standing in one of the last concession stands to be upgraded with the new units, Kanann was surprised to see the stadium head maintenance supervisor walk into the room; he was told he would be on vacation that day. "What the hell is going on in here, Bruce?" Supervisor Alan Wall asked.

"Sir, these are new refrigeration units for the stands," Alan answered back, then added, "I assumed you knew about this."

"Not at all!" the supervisor shouted back. "Let me see the paperwork!"

Handing over the clipboard with the invoices on them, Kanann said, "I just assumed you ordered these, boss."

While Wall paged through the invoices, he started shaking his head. Kanann looked at one of the appliance deliverymen and nodded his head toward his supervisor.

Kanann's boss just started to say, "No, no…" when from behind him a cupped hand covered his mouth and nose, preventing him from speaking or breathing. Wall's eyes opened wide and bugged out toward Kanann as a knife pierced his back, going deep into his heart. A few seconds later, the killer let him go and he dropped lifelessly to the ground.

Kanann told the killer, "Get rid of him, far from here, and make sure he's not found!"

With that, two of the deliverymen placed the lifeless body of Alan Wall into one of the empty appliance boxes and wheeled it to the empty delivery truck. Not even thinking twice about what had just happened, Kanann walked over to one of the other deliverymen and peered over his shoulder as he worked on the just-installed refrigeration unit. Looking down, he saw a digital timer connected to a battery supply and wires leading to several blocks of plastic explosives and a container the size of a small cooler with a radiation warning label on it. Putting his hand on the shoulder of the workman, Kanaan said, "Soon, my friend, soon."

Later that week in Washington, in the office occupied by supervisory agent James Hansen and members of his team, they were engrossed in going over the many daily threat assessments that come into their office, determining which might need more attention than others.

"Jim, there has been more traffic indicating New York in August, but we can't determine if it is the city or state," Agent Grafton reported.

"There has to be more than just one person involved in this," Agent Hansen said. "We have so many damn possible targets; let's just follow anything suspicious no matter how insignificant it seems."

Agent Hamilton walked quickly into the office with some paperwork, then said to Agent Hansen while handing it to him. "We were just notified by the New York State Police that they stopped a stolen semi-tractor trailer near Fresh Kills Park on the 440 in Staten Island, New York. They stopped it for not signaling a lane change, of all things. The driver got out of the truck, shooting at the officer, but was killed with return fire."

Agent Hansen looked at the paperwork and replied, "Why are they giving this to us?"

"The driver was of Middle Eastern descent with absolutely no identification," Agent Hamilton said. "In checking the back of the trailer, they found a dead body in a refrigerator delivery box. In fact, there were nine other empty refrigerator boxes in back.

And, one of their dogs found traces of an explosive scent in the back and their bomb disposal unit picked up slight traces of radioactivity."

"Shit! Hopefully we lucked out and this is what the chatter was about," Agent Hansen said as he picked up the phone to call the director. "Let's get our gear; we're heading to New York."

Five hours later, the team exited their black SUV at a secured maintenance lot at Fresh Kills Park, where the New York State Police had secured the semi-tractor trailer. Agent Hansen shook hands with Detective Stephen Remington from the New York State Police as he introduced himself. "Agent Hansen, the vehicle wasn't all that clean of evidence," Remington said. "I imagine they hadn't gotten to that point yet. We figure they probably planned to do that after dropping off the truck."

"Detective, what have you discovered yet?" Agent Hansen asked Remington.

"Agent, we know the truck was stolen two weeks ago from a terminal in Baltimore, Maryland. Our bomb and hazardous materials team detected the presence at some point of explosives and radioactive material in the trailer," Remington reported. "The body in one of the appliance boxes is that of a stadium maintenance supervisor, Alan Wall. He was supervisor of the entire MetLife Stadium in East Rutherford, New Jersey." He then added, "Because of the multiple states involved, the victim, the perp, and the bomb detection report, we thought possible terrorism and contacted the FBI."

"I'm afraid you might be right detective," Agent Hansen answered. Looking at Agent Grafton, he said, "Sue, contact the field office in Newark. Fill them in and tell them we are heading there to coordinate a response to MetLife Stadium. Have them send some undercover units to sit on the stadium till our team gets there to keep an eye on things."

Two hours later, the team was at FBI headquarters in Newark, meeting with the Bureau's regional SWAT and Bomb Disposal/ Hazardous Materials Response Team, planning a no-knock raid of the stadium for 9 p.m. Speaking to Agents Grafton and Hamilton, along with the leaders of the two FBI teams, Agent Hansen said, "We're going in without any warning and breaching four doors encompassing the stadium. We need speed and stealth, because we don't know if any suspected terrorists are there, but we must assume they are. There must be 20-plus concession stands in the stadium, so look in each one for the model number of the refrigerators we took off the boxes in the trailer. When you find one, don't touch it; secure it and radio your location so the EOD specialists can get to you."

It was a few minutes after 9 p.m. Eastern Time that the four access doors on each side of the stadium were breached and the teams slipped quietly into the stadium. Within minutes, all four teams reached and secured their first concession stand, but none contained the specific refrigerator. They radioed in their status and advised they were moving on the next one. Agents Hansen, Grafton, and Hamilton were with insertion team 2 almost at their third concession stand, when they confronted a maintenance supervisor coming out of the area. With about 20 feet between them, Agent Hansen yelled out, "FBI! Don't move. Identify yourself."

With his hands above his head, the man answered, "I'm night maintenance supervisor Bruce Kanaan. What is going on?"
The team leader motioned for Kanaan to lower his arms, which

he did as Agent Hansen asked, "We need your help in locating the concession stands. We have a reported threat. How many do you have working here tonight?"

Kanaan answered, "I have 10 other guys working tonight. Should I be worried?"

Hansen replied, "You will be okay. Can you let your men know we are here and searching the area? Have them all leave via their nearest exit point with their hands up and we will guide them away from the building."

Before Kanaan could answer, the echo of automatic gunfire rang through the deserted stadium walkways. Looking surprised, Kanaan pulled a 9mm handgun from the small of his back and fired into the squad of FBI agents, with Agent Grafton yelling out in pain. Almost simultaneously, multiple weapons were fired by the FBI team as Kanaan's body was riddled with bullets. The team leader then radioed out to all teams, "Assume all civilians are hostile."

Agent Hansen ran over to Agent Hansen along with the team paramedic. "Sue, where are you hit?" he asked.

"My thigh, Jim. I'm okay go on," Agent Hamilton answered as the paramedic treated her wound.

Then one of the other FBI agents yelled out, "we got one in here," as they discovered one of the refrigerators in the concession unit. Running into the area was a bomb specialist, who opened the side panel of the refrigerator, revealing the plastic explosive and box marked radioactive. "Holy shit," he said to himself as he reported back to the team.

Agent Hansen reported back to the command center and other teams that the refrigerators contained some type of nuclear dirty bomb. The operation continued for another two hours as teams swept the stadium, quickly taking out the other terrorists who were apparently assigned to guard the concession stands. When the all clear inside the stadium was given, Agent Hansen and Agent Hamilton exited and went over to the paramedic unit stationed at the mobile command center. They found Agent Grafton in back with an IV flowing into her left arm and an oxygen mask over her face. Moving it to the side, she said, "Hi Jim."

Agent Hansen answered back, "Hi Sue. How are you doing?"

"I'm good. The medic said it was a flesh wound. I should be out of the hospital tonight," Sue said with confidence.

The medic then came around and said, "Agents, we have to get to the hospital now."

Slapping the side of the ambulance, Agent Hansen said with a smile, "Sue, we did good. We stopped them. We all did good tonight."

With that, he slapped the back of the ambulance door again as it pulled away and walked over to the command post where Agent Hamilton was standing with the incident command team. "We just got damn lucky, damn lucky," Hanson said, then added, "We stopped them this time, but we know there are more out there, and the threats are getting more bold and closer together—more than the public realizes. I just feel it's going to get worse and it's leading to something even bigger."

A CHILLING DECEMBER

By 2020, there had been a notable uptick in radical and so-called lone wolf attacks on primarily soft targets within the continental U.S., along with several American assets abroad. There was an array of large, devastating attacks on various targets, including the attempt to set off dirty bombs at a late August NFL preseason game, a shooting at a public ice skating rink in Salt Lake City, an assault on a Memorial Day parade in Indianapolis, an airport luggage area attack in Dallas/Fort Worth International Airport, and an explosion at a Labor Day event in New York City. These were in addition to smaller and nonlethal attacks across the country.

Because of the attempted attack during an NFL preseason game, Special Supervisory Agent James Hansen's team became a Lone Wolf FBI Task Force, with its focus being to investigate the uptick, try to determine a pattern and develop a counterinsurgency program to combat it. In addition to the formation of this anti-terrorism task force, many laws—from local ordinances to state and federal regulations—had limited the types and number of personal weapons the public could own. The theory was if the public's access to firearms was reduced or eliminated, it would limit the weapons terrorists could use against the public and law enforcement officials.

It was now a chilly Christmas in 2020, even in Southern California, and nine years had passed since the meeting in Mosul where Sheda had laid out his plan for Haboob Wind. As Sheda's plan had stated, through the years, specific Islamic warriors had been called on to conduct terror attacks at unsuspecting locations around America and other Western countries. In all instances, warriors had sacrificed themselves in the name of Allah after inflicting unspeakable carnage among innocent civilians and first responders in multiple countries.

As predicted by Sheda, the public and governmental outcry had resulted in banning some semi-automatic weapons throughout the country. With each additional attack came more cries for gun control, increased dialog, and increased military action from numerous critics—and with that came more apathy as to the actual root cause of each attack. Today would be no different. This year alone—2020—had seen a large spike in the number of attacks both in the U.S. and against U.S. interests in Europe, with 11 such assaults already committed, six of them resulting in large numbers of dead and wounded.

So far, Wisconsin, in the heartland of the U.S., had escaped anything major because of these increased terror incidents. It was around 12:30 a.m. on a cold December morning just before Christmas in Stevens Point, Wisconsin, a small city known for its Point Brewery that was a true example of an all-American town. It boasted American flags and red, white, and blue decorations on every federal holiday; patriotism and Midwestern pride ran deep within the community. It also was the perfect place for the initial stages of Haboob Wind to take place—since it would be the last place in America anyone would suspect would harbor hidden hate that was about to bubble over into the heartland of America.

The chilled exhale of the crowd at the annual Christmas and holiday celebration looked as if it was a frozen cloud hovering semi-transparent over the revelers. The day had started off early with a parade downtown that included floats made by members of the community and local school bands from throughout the county—with Santa Claus in his sleigh surrounded by his elves on a farm trailer pulled by a local farmer's tractor bringing up the tail end. The parade concluded at a local park in Stevens Point where the festivities continued with a winter carnival, ice skating, and a Police vs. Fire Department hockey game, and it would end with an evening of local bands playing until the shutdown of festivities that was scheduled for one o'clock in the morning.

The last band of the night was three-quarters of the way through their last set when they made an announcement to the crowd, "We want to thank everyone for coming tonight. The Police Department wants you to finish up your beers! The park needs to start clearing out at 1 a.m. and please everyone be careful driving home. We all want to thank you all for coming out tonight."

At 12:47 a.m., Portage County Sheriff's Deputy Steve Mossholder advised the dispatcher that all was calm, and he didn't anticipate any issues with the crowds after the event. A few minutes later, the band had just started their last song when a loud bang was heard at the center left of the stage. The band abruptly stopped playing and there was an eerie silence over which the whimpering and crying of several people could be heard. The crowd slowly backed up in a semi-circle, revealing 10 obviously wounded individuals laying on the snow-covered ground. At the realization of what had happened, several women began screaming in horror. In front of them were so many dead and wounded holiday partiers who, only moments earlier, had been laughing, chatting, and singing along with the band. Some began to turn and attempted to run away but found it to be almost impossible with the number of people in the crowd behind them.

Slowly, one individual walked forward into the carnage. He had obviously just ended a phone conversation and placed the phone into his olive drab winter parka. He looked remarkably unshaken by what had just happened and had a strange smile on his face as he waded into the carnage. Almost as quickly as he'd put away his phone, he raised an AR-15 type rifle out from under his coat. While raising it to about waist high, he yelled out, "Allah Akbar" ("God is the greatest" in Arabic) and began to fire into the crowd.

Screams rang out as the bullets from this terrorist's weapon found their marks. After emptying his magazine, the terrorist ejected it onto the snow and reached for another in a vest he had on under the parka. The vest appeared to be black with numerous pockets containing several loaded magazines. Just as the shooter pulled back on the charging handle to load another round into the chamber, a deputy sheriff who was providing security had made his way to the open area in the crowd. With his weapon drawn, he yelled to the shooter, "Police! Drop your weapon!" In response, the shooter turned toward the deputy and pointed the rifle. The deputy fired off three rounds from his .45 caliber Glock service weapon. All three hit the shooter in the chest, only pushing him back a few inches. The officer then realized the shooter was wearing body armor and he started to dive behind a food stand for cover. Unfortunately, the shooter fired off four rounds, three of which hit the deputy in his vest, with the fourth hitting him in the head and killing him instantly.

As other officers tried to get through the crowd, they were getting reports that one of their own had been shot down. In the commotion of what seemed like many minutes, but was only seconds, the shooter didn't notice a man who was treating a woman with a gunshot wound to her right thigh as he continued to fire into the crowd, thinking of his options. This man was retired firefighter Captain Michael Donavon from Milwaukee, who was visiting family in Stevens Point over the holidays. He had only been enjoying his retirement for about three months. Besides being a retired firefighter, Michael had two other things that were going to help him and others survive this evening; he had spent nearly 30 years in the Army National Guard as an infantry officer with several combat deployments under his belt, and he held a CCW permit from the state of Wisconsin. Tucked in a shoulder holster was a .45 Caliber Colt Model 1911 A-1 pistol. It was like the one he had carried in the Army and had qualified as an expert with it.

Michael had observed the shootout with the deputy and it confirmed what he had assumed. This shooter had was wearing body armor and knew what he was doing. The precision of his firing and the ease at which he swapped out magazines told him this guy was experienced in close combat operations. It told him several things about what he had to do next. He needed to be fast, he needed to be accurate and it had to be a head shot—because he wouldn't get a second chance. Michael resorted to his combat arms training as he drew out his .45 and went into a roll to the side of the shooter. From about 10 yards away, he leveled his sights on the gunman's head.

Simultaneously, the gunman realized what Michael was doing and started to turn in his direction. In an automatic response, Michael fired one shot, hitting the shooter in his right temple, dropping him like a rock. Michael jumped up and ran over to the shooter and kicked the rifle away as he had done several times in Iraq and Afghanistan. He then placed his pistol at his feet and held his gold retirement shield over his head, waiting for the police officers to make their way to him and the dead shooter. As the officers approached, Michael he yelled out, "The shooter is down!"

It was now 12:57 a.m. The entire attack lasted only five minutes, but to those involved, it seemed like an hour. One of the officers asked Michael if he had seen anyone else. "I didn't see anyone else, but he was on his cell phone right before he started shooting. I noticed that because there was something about him that I found strange. It was like he seemed just too normal." Maybe it was from his dealings with the public while on the fire department in a large American city, or from his time in combat, but there was just something about the guy, Michael kept thinking to himself.

One of the officers got on his radio and requested dispatch to send fire and EMS. "We have multiple dead and wounded along with Unit 1217 being DOA! We need more units here 10-33," which in police code meant an extreme emergency.

The cold night air was pierced by the sound of sirens in the background and radio traffic. Three long tones—"Beeeeeeeeeep, Beeeeeeeeeep, Beeeeeeeeeep"—followed by, "Officers need assistance at the Stevens Point Holiday Carnival, shots fired, and officer down, and many civilians down, all units use tactical channel 3!"

It was 1:03 a.m. when the phone rang at the duty officer's desk at the FBI's Field Office in Milwaukee. Newly assigned FBI Agent William Anderson, the rookie on the team, ended up with some of the crappy assignments such as answering the phone in the middle of the night. He was stuck until he proved himself to the team, which would put him in a regular rotation—a practice not uncommon in most public safety units. Half-awake, Agent

Anderson answered the phone, "FBI Milwaukee Field Office Agent Anderson. How can I assist you?"

On the other end of the phone was the Portage County Sheriff William Harris. "Agent, this is Sheriff Harris, Portage County Sheriff's Office. We have a situation here! It appears we have had some type of terrorist attack at our annual Holiday Carnival in Stevens Point!"

Agent Anderson took down all the details, ending the call with, "Sheriff, thanks. We'll have a team right up there and I'll also notify Homeland and the ATF!" After hanging up, Agent Anderson's hand was shaking as he called the Supervising Agent of his field office, realizing terror had come to Wisconsin this Christmas.

Within hours, there were hordes of law enforcement and rescue personnel flooding into Stevens Point—and the significant presence of 24-hour news channels. Satellite trucks were everywhere, with numerous reporters giving viewers their take on the situation. Some even called this, "another act of senseless gun violence in America," totally ignoring or minimizing the reported shouts of "Allah Akbar" by the shooter before and during his short reign of terror. Before the dawn would break, there would be calls for even more of an increase in gun control measures beyond what had already been suggested and even passed into law, as well as a call for the complete banning of all semi-automatic weapons by politicians and certain members of the media—demands that were echoed by anti-2nd Amendment advocates. In what had become the automatic response, the 2nd Amendment advocates responded by saying the act of terrorism should be called what it is and reminded the interviewers that what had stopped this terrorist was a good guy with a gun.

But with the voices of the politicians, celebrities, and many liberal leaning citizens getting louder—calling for increased regulations on firearms—the laws would become more stringent within the states and the federal government. There would be several new bills introduced in the next few days and weeks to that effect, and some would be passed into laws that would be instrumental in the controlling the types of weapons and ammunition the public could possess.

This was progressing precisely the way Sheda had planned and it would be crucial to making Haboob Wind successful. His plan was to have enough small attacks across America and other Western countries involving the use of semi-automatic weapons in their execution that it would frighten the Americans and world citizenry into greatly reducing their numbers and reducing citizens' resistance to his planned invasion. As he had predicted, the anti-firearm forces in the U.S. were rising against the supporters of America's 2nd Amendment, resulting in successfully increased regulation and all-together banning of many firearms—the very firearms that could be used against his invading forces.

As the sun started to rise over the Sheda's hidden command center in Mosul, the television in the center was set to CNN in America. With a smirk, Sheda nodded his head "yes" as he heard of the successful attack in Wisconsin and reports of the increased chatter by the anti-firearm set to ban even more firearms—while refusing to accept the fact that terrorists don't follow America's gun laws. Looking to one of his brigade commanders, Sheda exclaimed, "Our plan is working!" This is the same comment he had repeated after each attack and the subsequent American news media reports over the years.

THE HUNT

Special Agent in Charge James Hansen (formerly Captain James Hansen of the Stonewall Brigade) had just arrived at the Anti-Terrorist Command Center at FBI headquarters in Washington. It was around 3 a.m., a little more than an hour since the terrorist attack had occurred in Stevens Point. It had been snowing heavily on his way in and although it seemed like it took him forever to get to the center, even running red lights and sirens, it was more like 25 minutes.

Walking into his office, he tossed his wet overcoat over the back of his chair and walked out into the situation room. The agent in charge of the Operations Center that night was Special Agent Larry Smith, who had been with the FBI for six years. His previous assignment was in counterintelligence before being assigned last month to the antiterrorism unit, which was really his specialty. He had been in Navy Intelligence, working at U.S. Central Command in the Middle East for four years following his graduation from U.S. Naval Academy in Annapolis in 2009. After leaving the Navy, Agent Smith applied to and was accepted into the FBI and made no mistake in letting the right people know he wanted to be in counterintelligence and antiterrorism someday. Since being with intelligence, he had been responsible for uncovering information on impending attacks and hidden terrorist cells that had led to their successful takedowns. His record was so impressive, in fact, that it had been long thought that he would eventually be working with the anti-terrorism unit in Washington.

Agent Smith handed Hansen a cup of hot black coffee, which he accepted saying, "Now bring me up to speed. What do we have?"

"Not much," Agent Smith stated. "We had absolutely no chatter of any type on this. All we know for right now is a white male with no identification, in his approximate mid-30s, set off some type of explosive device in front of a band playing at an annual holiday carnival. He then opened fire with a .223 caliber AR-15 into the crowd. There were numerous dead and wounded before a retired fire captain from the Milwaukee Fire Department took him down with a .45 with three shots, one to the head."

"No shit?" Hansen replied in his Virginia accent.

"Yes," Agent Smith replied. "Apparently, he had a CCW and was packing. He had spent 30 years in the Army National Guard in an infantry unit and retired as a Lieutenant Colonel. He had several tours in Iraq and Afghanistan before he retired from the guard."

"I like this guy already," stated Hansen. "Do you know I spent 20 years in the Virginia Army National Guard? I was one of the last units out of Iraq in 2011. I was fighting these fucking terrorists then and I still am. What else do we know?"

"Not a lot, just that he was loaded to bear. He had at least 20 magazines of 15 rounds each. He had three military-issue hand grenades and ATF on the scene suspect the initial blast was from a fourth. He was wearing body armor and apparently had some type of military training. ATF is running the serial number of the AR-15 and maybe we will get lucky, but we all know since semi-automatic weapons of that type were outlawed in 2018, the outcome might be iffy."

The agent was referring to the 2018 Anti-Crime Bill that banned many weapons, including assault-style weapons with detachable magazines. After passage of the law, anyone owning firearms of that type had 30 days to turn them over to a law enforcement agency for destruction. There were some heavy criminal penalties put in place for those who did not adhere to the new law. But in the haste to pass the new crime bill, it had tied the hands of law enforcement agencies.

"Well, we may get lucky," Hansen said, "with the serial number. It might only show it was sold years ago and had long disappeared from view until now.

"Fuck," he muttered. "Do you know when they passed this law they made it nearly impossible for us to track these fuckers down? Before the law, we could trace where the weapon was sold, when it was sold, by who, and to who! We could even find out if they used a range! Now they are all ghosts in the wind."

Agent Smith then told Hansen that witnesses had reported that the shooter had spoken to someone on a cell phone just after the explosion, prior to the shooting.

Hansen asked, "Anything from the phone?"

"Negative," replied Smith. "It had been a burner and the number he had called appeared to be another burner phone."

With a soft chuckle, SAIC Hansen shook his head and grimaced. "Now that is what should have been banned—burner phones."

"ATF and our regional evidence team have taken control of the scene and are processing it," the agent reported. "Homeland has set up a security perimeter around the park. Local and state law enforcement are searching for any vehicle that might have been left in the area. As soon as we hear anything, we'll let you know."

"Okay," SAIC Hansen confirmed. "I'm going to go into my office and make the White House aware of what we have. Let me know if anything else pops up." Hansen closed the door to his office behind him and settled in for a long day.

It was about 45 minutes before the door to Hansen's office opened again. He yelled out into the room, "Smith! Come in here please." Then, walking back to his desk, he sat down, opened a file folder and studied it.

Agent Smith entered the office and asked, "What do you need, boss?"

"Close the door and have a seat," ordered Hansen. "Larry, I see you spent four years in Navy Intelligence after the academy. You were in counterterrorism, right?"

"Yes sir. I did," replied Agent Smith.

Looking directly at Agent Smith, Hansen said, "Larry, when it is just us, it's Jim, okay?"

"Okay sir, umm sorry, Jim," Agent Smith replied with a chuckle.

"Well, that is one of the reasons I wanted you. You are ex-military, and from your reviews, you are good at what you do, Larry."

"Thanks Jim. What do we do now?" asked Agent Smith.

"Well, now this is a part of the job that you might not have realized," Hansen said with a small laugh. "Go home and pack enough stuff for about five days. We, my friend, are going to be in Milwaukee for at least that long, and we are wheels up at 0930."

"What about you, Jim?" asked Agent Smith.

"Me?" Hansen asked, a bit surprised.

"Sorry Jim, what about your clothes?" Agent Smith asked, a little embarrassed he had even brought it up.

"No worries, Larry. I keep a ready bag in my closet with enough in it for a week. Anything longer than that, well, that's what Wal-Mart is for."

SAIC Hansen explained further, "Ready bags, I'm sure you know what those are, sailor? I'd put one together and leave it in your office closet, Larry. I want you working with me on these incidents, and you're going to get a lot of frequent flyer miles in this unit."

"Roger that, Jim," Agent Smith said. "I'll go close my office and get my bag. I should be back in about an hour."

Agent Smith stopped at the office receptionist's desk and said, "I'm going to be in my office for a few minutes getting some things together. Then I'm running home for my travel bag; I guess we're going to Milwaukee. I should be back in about an hour."

Agent Smith slowly closed the door to his office and pushed the lock button. Sitting down at his desk, he opened a locked drawer, taking out an old Blackberry cell phone. He turned it on, sent a short text, and then powered it off and slipped it into the left inside breast pocket of his suit jacket. Walking over to his office door, he put his ear up to it and listened for a second. After assuring himself it was quiet, he walked over to his desk and from the same desk drawer, pulled out a prayer mat and placed it on the office floor. After taking off his shoes, Agent Smith knelt onto the mat and began to silently pray.

Smith then reflected on his journey from the U.S. Naval Academy to the elite FBI Anti-Terrorism Unit in Washington. Larry Smith was orphaned during his sophomore year of high school in the Village of Elk Grove, Minnesota, a suburb of Minneapolis. His appointment to the U.S. Naval Academy in his last few months of his senior year of high school gave him a way out of his foster home and into a new family with the Navy. His graduation with honors from the academy in 2009 was a true example of his determination and drive to become a U.S. Naval Officer and it didn't go unnoticed on several levels. The day after his graduation, newly commissioned Ensign Larry Smith spent one last night in Maryland before heading to the National Security Agency for specialized intelligence training. Smith treated himself to a fine dinner and a night in a plush Baltimore hotel before catching his ride in the morning for NSA headquarters. A knock on his hotel door at 10:20 p.m. interrupted him watching one of his favorite shows on the History Channel. Ensign Smith walked to the door and said, "Can I help you?"

A voice came from the other side of the door, "Hotel security. Ensign Smith, we need to talk to you."

Larry opened the door and was speechless when he was greeted by three men, one of whom looked so much like him, he had thought he was looking in the mirror. Two of the men were holding pistols aimed at him as one said, "Well, Mr. Smith, we have been waiting a very long time to meet you and we are quite the fans of your career and accomplishments."

Before he could respond, a muffled single shot was fired, and the life and career of the real Ensign Larry Smith had just ended and the new one had just begun. As two of the gunmen removed his body, Smith's replacement laid down in the hotel room bed and assumed his life.

His mind returning to present day reality, Agent Smith emerged from the elevator with his newly created go-bag. He made his way down the hallway toward the conference room next to the elevators.

Inside the conference room, SAIC Hansen was standing at the head of the conference table with four duplicate FBI file folders on the table, one for each member of the team heading to Milwaukee. Two other agents were waiting in the conference room and assigned to the same case in Wisconsin. Hansen made the introductions saying, "This is Agent Larry Smith, who's new to the unit. He has been with the bureau for six years. Prior to that, he was with U.S. Navy Intelligence after graduation from the U.S. Naval Academy in 2009. Larry, this is Special Agent Linda Hamilton. She is our forensic specialist with a specialty in terrorist explosives. She has been in the unit for three years and

10 years with the bureau." Pausing, he turned toward the other woman, "And this is our profiler, Agent Susan Grafton. She is good at what she does and has been in the unit for five years and 12 years with the bureau."

Agent Smith replied, "Agents, it is a pleasure to meet you both."

"Same here," they both replied.

"Each one of you please take a packet," Hansen said. "It has all the information we have collected so far from the terrorist attack in Wisconsin. Go over it on the flight and compare it with the other attacks we have had in the past. Look for any similarities or any type of crossovers, I don't care how minute it is."

Agent Grafton picked up her packet from the conference table and headed to the FBI SUV that would be taking them to the airport. With her being a profiler, she was always sizing up people and she'd gotten very good at reading people. When she had heard Agent Smith was a graduate of the U.S. Naval Academy and then went on to Naval Intelligence, it spiked her interest in her new teammate, since her own brother had also graduated from the U.S. Naval Academy in 2010.

Grabbing her packet, Agent Hamilton smiled at Hansen and Agent Smith, then also headed toward the SUV. After the four agents loaded their bags into

the back of the vehicle, they climbed in for their ride to the FBI hangar at Reagan International Airport. It had started snowing heavily again, causing the ride to take a little bit longer than usual. Hansen was in the front passenger seat of the SUV when he turned around and spoke to Agent Hamilton. "Linda, make sure you work with Larry on the flight to Milwaukee. During his time in Intelligence, he had a knack, almost sixth sense, with reading intelligence. That's why we were lucky enough to get him. I'm sure with your forensic knowledge and Larry's intelligence expertise, we might very well get a break with this case." With that, SAIC Hansen turned around and everyone stayed quiet for the rest of the ride.

NARROWING IN

The radio was on in the background, playing country music as the three airmen worked on the final touches of their restoration of their B-25, "American Pride." Looking up from the number two engine on the medium bomber, Stevo said to the others, "Man, we are so close to getting this thing done and ready for the final inspection. I can't wait to see her in the air."

Billy looked up from the front nose gear and replied with a big grin on his face, "Yup, a few more minor things after you are done Stevo, and this old gal is ready."

Billy and Freddie walked around the aircraft and inspected her new olive drab paint scheme and freshly applied early war stars. "Our next step in this new paint job is designing our nose art and reflecting the name we picked," Freddie said.

Stevo yelled down, "Did you hear that new crap in Wisconsin from last night?"

Billy replied, "Yeah, when is this crap going to be taken care of? It's like the fifth or sixth time this year just in the States alone."

"Well, we just need to take care of us and our families my friends," Freddie chimed in.

"Anyway, let's get back to what we can do. It's our plane so let's get our shit done!" boomed Steve. With that, the crew of American Pride decided the world would go on without their input and went back to work. As people walked between the hangars at the French Valley Airport, the soft melody of country music rolling out of the airmen's hangar was interrupted by someone yelling, "fuck!" followed by the metallic bang of a tool falling on the concrete floor. The sound represented another day in the life of a mechanic trying to restore a piece of history.

At the same time, nearly 2,600 miles away from the French Valley Airport, a U.S. government Gulfstream G550 jet owned by the FBI was approaching Milwaukee International Airport. On board was Agent Hansen's team, coming to investigate the previous day's attack in Stevens Point. The SAIC was still studying the case files from the latest attack and comparing it to the previous attacks in the U.S. earlier that year. He whispered to himself, "I know it's here. Something is here linking them all together. I just can't see it yet."

Agent Smith was doing the same thing, going over the previous and current files, but his observations were for a different purpose. As from his days with Naval Intelligence, he would uncover just enough information to bring praise and even promotion upon him, but simultaneously steer investigators in a different and wrong direction, away from the facts in the case.

Agent Hamilton was peering into her laptop screen, going over pictures of each scene and the different forensic reports, looking for anything to break through these attacks. However, Agent

Grafton just sat there and stared at Agent Smith with a small smile on her face. It didn't go unnoticed by Agent Smith, who closed his laptop screen rapidly and looked at her. "Yes?" he said, obviously annoyed with her. However, Agent Grafton remained silent. "What? Are you profiling me?" asked Agent Smith.

Agent Grafton replied, "Not really. Just sizing you up. I did the same thing to my brother and it always pissed him off. Did you know my brother, Lieutenant Commander Charlie Grafton? He graduated the year after you from the Naval Academy and went into Naval Intelligence, but with CINCPAC," Agent Grafton added.

"No. I don't know him," replied Agent Smith, thinking to himself, "fuck."

"I just wondered," she said. "I told him about you. He didn't know you, either. He is home right now in Green Bay on leave. I hope we can all meet up."

Agent Smith just said, "Yeah, I hope so."

Hansen was in the back of the plane at its small galley getting another cup of coffee when Agent Grafton went back and grabbed an empty coffee mug. "I imagine you overheard that?" she asked.

"Yes, and?" he replied.

"I don't know; there is just something about him, sir. I'm not sure—maybe it's my profiling psyche," she said with a chuckle. "I lied, also. My brother does remember him, but he is nothing like how my brother described him."

"Hmm, interesting, woman's intuition I guess. Well, just keep me informed, and quietly. He is new here and maybe that is all it is—the new kid on the block syndrome," Agent Hansen pondered aloud.

Oh, by the way, I need to show you a really good cup of coffee one of these days," Agent Grafton said with a smile as she turned back into the cabin area.

"Ah, okay," Agent Hansen replied with a small smile as they both walked back to their seats to finish up research, because they would be landing in about 45 minutes.

Agent Hamilton looked up from her evidence reports. She was holding several in both hands and said, "This might be nothing, but I found something strange on each of the past terrorist attacks this last year, including the one in Wisconsin."

"What did you find, Agent Hamilton? I've been pouring over everything thinking I was missing something obvious," said Agent Hansen.

"Sir, it would be easy to miss because it looks so normal on each report separately," Agent Hamilton replied.

Agent Smith and Agent Grafton chimed in with, "Well, what did you find?"

"What I have on the first incident last March was eight minutes prior to the attack, a sector police unit in the area reported to dispatch and other units that the area was secure," Agent Hamilton reported.

"That's normal police work and nothing more," retorted Agent Smith.

Agent Hamilton responded, "Yes, I agree, but looking at the police logs for each other incident, including this latest one, an area police unit reported to dispatch that their areas, which included the attack sites, were secure. In each instance, reports were eight to 12 minutes prior to the attack."

Agent Hansen stood up, walked over to Agent Hamilton and looked at the incident logs. "Shit! I was in the Army and those are synchronized recon reports, especially all at the same time," he said.

Agent Smith chimed in with, "I'm sure it is just a fluke coincidence, and good beat police work."

Agent Hansen gave Agent Smith a quick scowl and said, "Agent Smith, you are new here and there are no coincidences until we determine there are!"

Agent Smith then started to reply, "I was only..." when SAIC Hansen looked directly at him.

"Enough, look at last year's incidents, and then the year before, etc. and see if there is anything similar. And I mean ASAP!"

Agent Hamilton looked at both Agent Hansen and Agent Grafton and said, "They may have not only been advising dispatch that everything was clear, but also telling the terrorists it was all clear to strike."

"Exactly!" Agent Hansen replied and then added, "If that is true, we've been infiltrated and who knows how far it goes and into what agencies."

Agent Hansen was just about to say something else when the pilot announced they were on final approach into Milwaukee and everyone should take their seats. Hansen informed the team, "I'm going to fire off a couple emails and set up a meeting as soon as we get to the Field Office." The team then began to ready themselves for the landing.

Agent Smith stood up and said, "Well, I better hit the head now then," and walked aft to the lavatory.

Shortly after Agent Smith had gone into the lavatory, the intercom rang in the passenger area. Agent Grafton answered the handset and was told the pilot wanted to speak to Agent Hansen. Handing the phone to Agent Hansen she said, "It's for you sir."

Agent Hansen was only on the intercom for a few seconds and said, "Okay, thanks," before hanging up the handset. He stood up, walking over to Agent Grafton and whispering into her ear, "I want to talk to you in in private when we get to the field office, and just nod." Agent Grafton nodded as Agent Hansen sat back down and buckled his lap belt.

Shortly after that, Agent Smith walked back into the passenger area and with a smile, sat down in his seat and bucked his lap belt. The rest of the team finished up on their tablets and readied for their arrival.

It was a cold and snowy evening as the government G550 taxied over to a secured parking area on the tarmac near the flight operations of the Wisconsin Air National Guard 128th Air Refueling Wing (ARW). Waiting for them was a black GMC Suburban with U.S. government plates. Standing next to the vehicle was its driver, Agent William Anderson and the SAIC Allen Fredrick. Anderson opened the rear passenger doors as Frederick shook Agent Hansen's hand, welcoming him and his team to Milwaukee. After everyone was settled in the SUV, it pulled away from the tarmac, headed toward downtown Milwaukee and the FBI Field Office.

Agent Frederick turned to his left and over his shoulder said to Agent Hansen, "Jim, we have a conference room ready and our forensic team supervisor, representatives from the ATF, the Wisconsin Justice Department, and a captain from the Portage County Sheriff's Department where Stevens Point is located are all waiting." Agent Hansen nodded his head in acknowledgement and then stared out the SUV's snow-spotted window, pondering the events that unfolded on the flight.

It was about 20 minutes after eight in the evening as the FBI team from Washington walked into the conference room at the Field Office. As greetings and handshakes were exchanged, Agent James Hansen noticed that over in one corner of the room was a man in a Portage County sheriff's captain's uniform looking distraught as he was talking in almost a whisper on a cell phone. The captain was Geoffrey Lindsey, and upon seeing the FBI team enter the conference room, he hurriedly ended the conversation and walked over to James Hansen, holding out his hand and introducing himself. The captain followed up the introduction with, "I'm sorry for that, but I just got some bad news that one of our newer deputies was just shot and killed during a traffic stop northwest of Stevens Point."

"Damn, captain. I'm so sorry. Any details yet?" Agent Hansen asked.

"Not really, Agent Hansen. Everything is just preliminary right now," the captain frowned.

Agent Hansen grimaced and went on, "How tragic. Do you know who the deputy was?"

"Yes, Deputy Steve Mossholder, who's only been with us for a little under two years," Captain Lindsey replied. An astonished look came over Agent Hansen's face, realizing that was the name of the deputy who had reported the attack area all clear prior to the attack.

"Captain, would you mind going to the communications center here and getting a hard copy of the shooting information, at least what you have so far?" Agent Hansen asked.

"Do you think it is related?" Captain Lindsey asked.

"I don't know. It could be; everything is suspect now. Agent Smith, go with the captain and make sure we don't need anything else," Agent Hansen ordered.

As the captain and Agent Smith walked out of the conference center, Agent Hansen took Agent Grafton by the arm, leading her into a corner of the room. "Why did you send Agent Smith with the captain when the captain can get the info himself?" Agent Grafton asked right away.

"I wanted him out of the room and this is the face-to-face I wanted, a little impromptu, but current events warrant it," he replied. "I'm calling on your intuition, which might not be far off, Agent Grafton. The call I got from the pilot was telling me of a cell signal going out from the plane," Agent Hansen said in a hushed tone. "It was after Agent Smith went into the lavatory. Now we find out this deputy is dead. I suspect the deputy's death came after the cell call left our plane. If we have sleepers, it is looking possibly like Agent Smith is one of them."

Agent Hansen added, "I want you to step out and call your brother. Ask him if he will come to Milwaukee. Then come back into the room and let Agent Smith know your brother is coming to visit you while we're here. I suspect Agent Smith will get nervous." Agent Hansen then stepped back from Agent Grafton, who nodded and walked out of the conference room.

Agent Hansen then turned and walked over to the Milwaukee field office supervisor and asked to talk to him in his office alone. Ten minutes later, Agent Hansen and Milwaukee Agent Frederick walked back into the conference room along with two other Milwaukee agents who were carrying cardboard file boxes. Captain Lindsey and Agent Smith had returned already and had with them numerous pages of typed paper that they were both looking at and talking about. Shortly thereafter, Grafton entered the room with a smile on her face. Walking over to Agent Smith, she excitedly said, "I've got some great news! My brother is in Milwaukee and on his way over. He is anxious to meet you and he wanted me to tell you he can't wait to compare stories from the Naval Academy!"

All eyes in the room drifted over to Agent Smith, who replied with what sounded like forced enthusiasm, "Awesome! I can't wait to meet him! When will he be here?"

"In about 45 minutes. He is in Waukesha right now," Agent Grafton answered.

"Maybe we can go out for a drink later tonight then? But I had one too many cups of coffee on the flight here and I must hit the head again," Agent Smith said as he started to turn and head out to the hallway.

Agent Smith was about two feet from the hallway door when he heard, "Freeze, Larry!" an order in the booming voice of Agent Hansen, a trained Army infantry officer turned FBI agent.

Turning halfway around, Agent Smith saw at least six FBI Glock service pistols aimed at his torso. Agent Smith had a smile and with a soft laugh reached for his own Glock service weapon. He hadn't even gotten within six inches of it when numerous .45 caliber rounds hit his chest and abdomen from the other agents' weapons. Agent Smith fell to the ground, his service weapon falling out of his holster and landing about a foot from his left hand. As Agent Smith lay there bleeding to death, Hansen ran over to him and kicked his Glock out into the hallway. Kneeling next to him, Hansen asked, "Why Larry? Why?"

Turning his face slightly to look Hansen directly in the eyes, he said, "Allah Akbar," then went motionless.

Looking stunned, Agent Hansen searched Agent Smith's suit coat pockets, discovering a non-government-issued Blackberry cell phone.

Standing up holding the Blackberry, he turned to his forensics expert, Agent Linda Hamilton, handed the Blackberry to her and said, "Hamilton, see what you can find out about this." Then looking at Agent Grafton, he said, "Grafton, when your brother gets here I want him to look at Agent Smith and see if he can identify him. I'm assuming he won't be able to."

The three of them then walked out into the hallway, where Agent Frederick was on his cell phone reporting on the situation to Washington and motioning them to come over. As they walked toward Agent Frederick, the Milwaukee FBI's forensic team entered the conference room to process this new crime scene. Agent Frederick finished the call and looking at the team asked, "What the fuck just happened, Jim?"

"I'm not sure, Allen, but we better put on a pot of fresh coffee and settle into your office. I have a feeling this is the start of a lot of late nights, and I've come up with one hell of a hypothesis my friend," Agent Hansen quipped as the four of them headed to Agent Frederick's office.

The phone rang in Agent Frederick's office at 10:20 p.m., indicating that Agent Grafton's brother had just arrived and was in the lobby. Agent Grafton led the way into the foyer and embraced her brother, then turned to introduce him to the others. "Agent Hansen, Agent Frederick, Agent Hamilton, this is my brother, Lieutenant Commander Charles Grafton."

With the introductions done, Hansen was asking Commander Grafton about his time at the Naval Academy and his interactions with his classmate Larry Smith. Heading into Frederick's office, the five sat down at a conference table in the room. Commander Grafton told the agents from what he remembered of Midshipman Smith, he was an outgoing, friendly classmate who absolutely loved the Minnesota Vikings. He'd played high school football in suburban Minneapolis and outside of his foster parents, he had no other family. He also said the last time he'd seen Larry was the evening after graduation and they really had not been in contact since.

Handing an FBI file to Commander Grafton, Agent Hansen said, "Commander this is Agent Larry Smith's file and we would like you to look at it."

Opening the file, he looked at the personnel pictures of Agent Smith along with pictures of him in his Navy Whites while a member of Naval Intelligence. Looking up at Agent Hansen, Commander Grafton said, "Agent Hansen, I don't know who this is, but I do know it's not the Larry Smith I knew." He then added, "There are some similarities, but that is about it." Commander Grafton asked, "Have you checked with his foster parents in Minneapolis?"

"We tried," Agent Hansen replied, "but his foster parents were killed in a traffic accident the day after his graduation from the Naval Academy, on their way home." The FBI team and Lieutenant Commander Grafton talked for about 20 more minutes before he left, with his sister escorting him out of the office building.

Looking at the remaining agents, Agent Hansen queried, "How deep does this go? My thoughts have been going to the fact that we have infiltration indications in local law enforcement and now in our office. We need to double our security efforts and restrict our office's exposure to other teams until everyone is properly vetted. We don't know how deep this goes, but it is the buildup to either a major incident within the continental U.S. or a series of them."

Agent Grafton returned to the office and Hansen advised them all they would be wheels up at 8 a.m. tomorrow for Washington and they would need a private meeting with the FBI Director on this.

Agent Hansen's team assembled back in the office by 3:30 p.m. the next day and headed almost immediately to the FBI Director's office to explain what their investigation had uncovered over the last 24 hours. After a nearly three-hour meeting, Agent Hansen and his team had the authorization to form their own handpicked domestic anti-terrorism unit. Under the name DART, a new government acronym that stood for Domestic Anti-Terrorism Response Team, they had the authority to consider local, state, and federal agencies for any indications of infiltration by terrorists.

It was in the early morning hours of September 9, 2021 in the desert south of Temecula, California in Riverside County that Border Patrol Agent Samuel Vazquez was sitting in his patrol unit. On a deserted dirt side road, southeast of Temecula in the Wine Country with his headlights out, he listened to the chatter of the Border Patrol radio while sipping a cup of very hot black coffee.

Then out of the darkness, on a southbound road near where he was parked, a dark-colored SUV appeared and sped past his location with its headlights off. Instinctively, Agent Vazquez got on his radio and advised the dispatcher of his pursuit and the little information he had while simultaneously turning on his emergency lights and siren. Vazquez constantly gave a position update as speeds in his chase got up to near 90 mph on back roads.

Unable to make an out a license plate, in the distance he saw the lights of his backup units heading toward him. Seeing the responding police units in front of him, the driver of the speeding car turned sharply to the left, attempting to go off road into a vineyard. He lost control of the SUV in the gravel and rolled over several times in a cloud of dirt and dust before coming to a stop right side up.

Agent Vazquez bolted from his patrol unit with his 12-gauge pump shotgun aimed at the SUV. He ordered everyone out of the vehicle with their hands up. By this time, other officers were approaching from the other side of the vehicle with their service weapons trained on the SUV, shouting out similar orders to the occupants. In an instant, the driver's rear passenger door flew open, along with the two passenger doors on the passenger's side. Three males emerged with what appeared to be AK-47 rifles. Instinctively, all officers opened fire at the same time, killing the three gunmen before they could engage the Border Patrol agents. A voice came from the driver's side of the SUV, "Don't shoot! I'm coming out!" as a handgun flew out the window and the door opened slowly. The subject was ordered to the ground as Agent Vazquez approached the driver and handcuffed him behind his back while other agents provided cover. Agent Vazquez and another officer pulled the driver to his feet as the other agents opened the back of the SUV, finding a stash of equipment.

Walking to the back of the SUV, one of the other agents said, "Vazquez, look at this." The back of SUV contained a cache of automatic weapons, ammunition, radios, binoculars, military maps of the area, multiple USMC camouflaged uniforms, and law enforcement uniforms, all on top of a stack of some type of metallic tarps. A supervising border agent advised their dispatcher to have the ATF and FBI come to the scene ASAP.

Agent Vazquez handed his supervisor the contents of his prisoner's pockets, which consisted of only a wallet and a key with a tag imprinted with #256 at the Safe and Tight Storage in Hemet, California.

Opening the wallet of the driver, the supervising agent only could ask, "What the fuck?" as it displayed the badge of a deputy sheriff from the Imperial County Sheriff's Department and a department identification card that was the drivers based on its picture of Deputy Sheriff William Butterfield. The supervising agent looked at the driver and asked, "What the hell is going on?"

The driver replied, "This is where I ask for a lawyer," and he shut up.

"What is this key for?" the supervisory agent asked.

The driver only laughed and said one word, "Lawyer."

The supervising agent's cell rang. It was the supervisory agent from the San Diego Field Office of the FBI. They talked for a bit and the supervisory agent filled in the FBI of what they had and about the key to this storage unit. After about five minutes, the Border Patrol supervisor returned to the back of the SUV and said the FBI wanted the driver taken ASAP to March Air Reserve Base in Riverside, where several agents would be waiting for him. In the meantime, the other Border Patrol agents would secure the SUV and wait for the FBI and ATF teams to arrive.

It was near nine in the morning Eastern time on September 9, 2021, nine months after the incident involving Agent Larry Smith in the Milwaukee Field Office, when Agent Hansen sat on the phone, jotting down some notes on his legal pad at the DART headquarters in Washington. Hanging up the phone, he called Agents Grafton and Hamilton into his office. Accompanying them was Special Agent William Anderson, who had been with the Milwaukee Field Office originally and was one of the agents who helped take down Agent Larry Smith the previous year. He'd worked so well with the team, that he was asked to join them in May 2021.

"So, folks, do you have your go bags ready?" Agent Hansen asked. "We are heading to California for maybe a week."

"What's up?" Agent Grafton asked.

Agent Hansen brought them up to speed. "As we all know, the CIA, NSA, and about every other acronym in federal law enforcement community has been tracking down the information gathered off Agent Larry Smith's Blackberry and his computers," he said. "Every officer who had given a status report prior to an attack has either disappeared or was killed while on duty, so that left a dead end. We're thinking all of them were sleepers and we don't know for how long. However, they were converted at some point and we had found documentation to support that fact during the investigations."

Then Agent Hansen looked up at the wall and said, "As for Agent Larry Smith, yes Larry Smith! We have no idea who the fuck he really was, but he wasn't the real Larry Smith and DNA has confirmed that. His autopsy showed extensive facial plastic surgery, and it was good." Then he added, "We will find out though, somehow."

Agent Hansen moved on. "But now for California," he began. "All the data we've gathered from these subjects points nowhere because everyone involved is dead. Cleaning up loose ends, I would assume. The CIA and the NSA have picked up on something around the 20th anniversary of 9/11 and we think these incidents, including the sleepers, are leading up to it. The speculation is possibly an attack on Los Angeles or in that vicinity, maybe even Hollywood. Something that will make international news and bolster their propaganda and recruitment."

Agent Hansen expanded, "We may have just got a break—maybe a link to all this and the major incident we have feared. I just got off the phone with the Field Office in Los Angeles. Last night, the Border Patrol stopped four individuals in the desert southeast of Temecula, California after a high-speed chase and a shootout ensued. The driver survived."

Standing up from his desk and walking over to a map of the U.S., he pointed at Southern California and said, "The three who were killed appear to be of Middle Eastern descent. The driver is one William Butterfield, a deputy with the Imperial County Sheriff's Department south of Riverside County. They had automatic weapons in the back of the SUV. Also, they recovered ammunition and several SAT phones along with other portable radio equipment, tactical maps, and police and military uniforms." Hansen then continued, "There were also these tarps and we are not sure what they are for. They appear to be some type of metallic woven material. In addition, Butterfield had a key to a storage locker in Hemet, California. Local law enforcement and our regional field offices for the FBI and ATF raided it shortly after the arrest. It was a cache of weapons, more of these tarps, radio equipment, more military uniforms, and multiple police agency uniforms. Now Butterfield seems to be wavering a bit after first lawyering up and he is the nut I think we can now crack! Most importantly, he is still alive!"

Placing the paperwork into his briefcase, Agent Hansen said, "They are holding him in a special detention area at the Customs Enforcement Office at the March Air Reserve Base in Riverside. So, that's where we're headed. We're going to set up an operations center there and start with a more intense interrogation of Butterfield. The California Air National Guard has a drone unit there and a satellite surveillance command center that will be at our disposal. We are wheels up in about an hour. Let's move!"

THE STORM
BEGINS

The DART's G550 was somewhere over Missouri when Hansen was advised that the subject in custody at March Air Reserve Base was showing some willingness to talk, but only to the person in charge. In finishing his conversation with one of the FBI interrogators at U.S. Customs holding him at March, Hansen said, "Okay, sounds good. Get him something he likes to eat, and we'll be there in about four hours."

Since leaving for California, the team had been pouring over all the material recovered in Temecula and Hemet, in addition to a copy of Deputy Butterfield's Sheriff's Department personnel file. Looking at the team, the special agent in charge said, "Butterfield is willing to talk, but he only wants to speak to me. I'm hoping it's a crack in all of this. You all have anything new?"

Agent Grafton, looking up from Butterfield's file, said, "I can't see a thing. He's been with the Sheriff's Department for around two years, an exceptional officer with a wife and two kids living in El Centro, California."

Agent Anderson added, "The contents of the SUV and the storage locker point to preparedness for some type of attack in which either law enforcement, the military, or possibly both are the target. The uniforms, identification cards and processing equipment indicate that's the most likely scenario."

Agent Hamilton chimed in, "In looking at the maps and other papers, nothing really stands out. However, within the map area there are multiple military installations, power plants and a desalination project underway at the Salton Sea. But we have the closed San Onofre Nuclear Generating Station, which still has spent radioactive material being stored. This one scares me."

Taking it all in, Hansen said, "Okay, take another look then get some rest. We'll be in Riverside in about four hours and this will probably be a long night." Then, looking over toward Agent Anderson, Hansen added, "Relay our threat assessment to the LA Office and have them advise security at those locations to be extra vigilant, especially with any personnel who don't seem right."

The team's G550 touched down at March Air Reserve Base around 7:20 p.m. PST and taxied toward the U.S. Customs operations center near the airfield's control tower. They entered the conference room at the U.S. Customs office and met with the FBI's interrogation team that had been interviewing and monitoring Deputy Butterfield. The FBI's lead integrator was Special Agent Lester Wright, a 25-year veteran of the FBI who had been an interrogator since 2005. "Anything new Lester?" Hansen asked.

"No, not really, but he did give up on his lawyer request if he could talk to you, Jim," Wright said.

"Okay, give me about 15-20 minutes to look at your notes and I'll go in and talk to him," Hansen replied.

The door to the interrogation room opened and in walked James Hansen, followed by Lester Wright. Shackled and looking up from a table in the center of a very stark room, Deputy Butterfield looked up and asked, "You the guy in charge?"

Hansen replied, "Yes, I'm Special Agent in Charge James Hansen. I'm head of the FBI's Domestic Anti-Terrorism Response Team. You wanted to talk to me?"

Deputy Butterfield immediately began to sob, saying, "I'm a good cop. I don't know what to do. They got my wife and kids. You have to find them. Please!"

Looking semi-shocked, Hansen replied, "Okay, okay, we will. Tell me what happened."

With tears in his eyes, Deputy Butterfield said, "About three weeks ago, I was approached while on duty. A guy handed me a picture of my wife and kids at the park, a picture that had crosses over each of their faces."

Hansen asked, "Do you know where they are now?"

"Last I heard, at our house in El Centro," Deputy Butterfield said. "I don't know if they are alone, alive or dead. I haven't seen or talked to them in five days. I've been with those guys the Border Patrol killed."

Looking at Agent Wright, Hansen said, "Get some people over to the deputy's house, now." Looking back at Butterfield, he said,

"We'll take care of them and as soon as we hear something, I'll let you know. Now what did they want with you, deputy?"

"I don't really know. They spoke English but with what seemed like Middle Eastern accents, and in another language I didn't recognize when they spoke to each other," Deputy Butterfield replied. "I'll tell you that they are vicious, and I've seen them kill without any emotion. They had me rent that storage locker in Hemet and get them uniforms from the Imperial County Sheriff's Department."

Hansen then asked, "Do you know the target?"

"No, I don't," Deputy Butterfield said. "They seemed excited about the Navy bunkers at Seal Beach and the Marine Air Wing at Miramar, but whatever it is, it's soon, because they kept referencing the 11th."

"What about the desert near Temecula?" Hansen then asked.

Deputy Butterfield replied, "They had me drive out there and leave a pile of those blankets, a radio, and some rifles. But I never saw anyone else at the location where we dropped them off."

"Oh, one more thing," Hansen said. "If you were being held, how did you happen to have the pistol you tossed out the window when you were arrested?"

"I managed to take it from the storage locker and hide it on me before we left," the deputy said." If you look at the magazine, it's empty because I couldn't get to the ammunition."

"Okay, deputy, thank you," Hansen said. "I'll let you know what we find out about your family as soon as I hear. If you behave yourself, I'll have the shackles taken off," to which Deputy Butterfield nodded in agreement.

Hansen went back to the conference room and met with the rest of team. "If he is telling us the truth, all we know is there will be some type of attack in Southern California sometime on September 11th."

Looking at Wright, Hansen asked, "What about the gun he had?"

Agent Wright confirmed, "It was unloaded, Jim."

It was silent for a short time when the phone in the conference room rang and Agent Grafton picked it up and took a message. Looking at Hansen, she said, "Imperial County Sheriff's Department says Butterfield's wife and kids are okay, and according to his wife, she has had no idea where he's been for the last five days."

◇ ◇ ◇

It was 08:00 hrs. on September 11, 2021 at Cheyenne Mountain, Colorado, five and a half hours before the opening strike of Haboob Wind. It had been almost 11 years since the initial briefing was given to senior ISIS leadership by General Sheda. A critical portion of the plan necessary for its success was the use of sleeper cells that were in place within the American framework—in some cases for up to 15 years. Many of these sleepers had worked their way into trusted positions of authority within civilian and military organizations. These sleepers were so hidden within the framework of American society that even their closest family members had no idea of their affiliation with this terrorist organization.

In his office in cybersecurity at Cheyenne Mountain, Lieutenant Colonel Ali Fayed came out of his office sipping on a cup of black coffee from his favorite travel mug. The mug had been given to him by his wife of 16 years and it held the picture of his son in his high school football team. Looking at the clipboard, he walked over to a Technical Sergeant who was sitting at his terminal in the Colonel's office. "Sergeant, can you go down to the operations center and tell Major Graves I would like to talk to him? He isn't answering his phone."

"Yes, sir," replied the Technical Sergeant, getting up and walking out of the office.

After seeing the sergeant go around the hallway corner, Colonel Fayed unscrewed the bottom of his coffee mug and exposed a small USB flash drive. Looking around once more, he placed the drive into the open port on the front of the sergeant's computer. It took less than 20 seconds for a specially designed virus to be uploaded into the computer's mainframe. This virus—created by the North Korean government cyber espionage division—was designed to rapidly spread within the secure system, leaving no trace of its presence and leaving no trail of its path. As a result, it would make the ICBM surveillance and early warning system at Cheyenne Mountain blind to any such launch and flight pattern from the North Korean peninsula.

This was an act that had been repeated in other American military and surveillance commands by other sleeping ISIS agents—resulting in the United States of America being totally blind to North Korean activity.

It was 1512 hrs. in Brooklyn, New York as NYPD patrol unit David 27A left the secure lot to the side of the precinct to start its 3-11 p.m. patrol shift. It was a hot September 11 in 2021 and the officers of David 27A figured it would be a busy, hot night. David 27A was manned by Officers David Williamson and Matt Bennet.

Williamson was driving this shift and Bennet was working the radio as they went on their first call of the day, a family disturbance. It was a rather mundane call and they were able to clear it right away.

While continuing their patrol, they took part in their usual bantering, which they had done for the last four years working patrol together. They talked about everything from what they had done on their days off to their baseball playoff hopes— Williamson was a Mets fan and Bennet was a Yankees fan.

Approximately two and a half hours later, Williamson and Bennet had just cleared their fifth call of the shift—a noise complaint from an elderly couple that was watching reruns of Perry Mason and was interrupted by kids setting off firecrackers next to their brownstone. Both were chuckling over the call as they pulled away when Officer Williamson received a text on his phone. Williamson looked at the screen briefly and placed the phone back in the holster on his utility belt. Williamson's face turned from a smile over the last call to a very solemn look. Officer Bennet asked, "Is everything okay?"

Williamson looked over to Bennet and said, "You know I think a lot of you and our friendship, especially after the past four years."

Bennet, looking at Williamson said, "Don't tell me you're breaking up with me?" laughing at the statement.

"No but this pains me so much!" said Williamson. Then, drawing his Glock service weapon and pointing it to Bennet's face, startling Bennet, he chanted, "Allah Akbar, my friend" and fired the weapon into Bennet's face, killing him instantly.

Williamson then picked up the microphone in the patrol unit and said, "David 27A show us 10-6 for dinner."

"10-4 David 27A," replied the dispatcher.

Williamson drove his patrol unit to a secluded salvage yard in the district next to his. Pulling into the parking lot, he saw 11 other patrol cars, four fire department medical units and three fire engines. To the left of them in the far corner of the salvage yard, he saw a pile of bodies of other eliminated coworkers and the staff of the salvage yard. He knew the body of his partner and friend would soon be with them.

A man with a scraggly beard wearing blue jeans and a black polo shirt instructed him to pull up closely to the other patrol cars. Two of the medics opened the back of one of the medical units and started dispersing large tarps to the remaining police officers and firefighters. These were a specially designed Faraday tarps that had been smuggled into the country to be placed over equipment that was to be protected from the EPW detonation. The man with the beard was barking orders to hurry and he was obviously in charge, Williamson assumed, since everyone was in so deep no one knew who the other members of the cells were until they were given the text message to meet at predesignated sites after eliminating their partners or coworkers.

After all the vehicles were covered, the man in the beard began to explain how they would eliminate threats to the invasion under the color of their authority until the invading forces could link up with them.

This scene and procedure was not unique. It was repeated in other locations around the city of New York and through major metropolitan areas across the country in the hours prior to the detonation of the EPW and subsequent invasion of the United States.

It was late morning at Fort Irwin, California, nearing 1130 hrs., and the crew of Thunder 190, a U.S. Army Abrams Main Battle Tank, was heading out for gunnery practice with a full load of HEAT (High Explosive Anti-Tank) and smoke munitions. First Lieutenant Alfred Washington told the driver he wanted to stop out by the Monument Rock before heading to the range. He told the driver his wife wanted to give him something and it could not wait until later. It was not unusual for the tankers to stop by the rock memorial and meet family, so the driver and crew didn't think a thing about it. The rock memorial was a special and sacred area for Army personnel, especially cavalry troopers. It was created and maintained by the troopers to track the history, deployments, and losses of various units that had passed through Fort Irwin.

The Abrams Thunder 190 parked about 50 meters east of the monument as the lieutenant's wife's SUV approached the tank. The lieutenant told his crew to get out and take 10 and he'd be back shortly. Lieutenant Washington walked over to the SUV as his crew was talking, some having a smoke and others drinking water at the back of the tank. In an instant, three men in U.S. Army BDUs jumped out of the SUV and machine gun fire broke out from the back of the SUV aimed toward the back of the parked tank. When the smoke cleared, the crew of Thunder 190 lay sprawled by the treads, dead and dying. The three men then removed a large tarp from the back of the SUV and began running toward the Abrams tank to cover it with Faraday protection. "Hurry!" yelled Lieutenant Williams. "We only have a few minutes!"

Within minutes, the tank was covered. Just like the public safety agencies in New York City, this scene was repeated at various military bases across America in a similar fashion.

It was approximately 1230 hrs. at the U.S. Customs office at March Air Reserve Base when forensic specialist Agent Linda Hamilton looked up from her desk and focused on a poster by the bulletin board. Agent Hamilton slowly walked over to the poster and read about an upcoming area air show. Ripping it from the wall, she ran into the conference room yelling, "Jim, it was right there in front of us. The El Centro Air Show is today with its 20th anniversary tribute to 9/11! It's an open base today and it's in Imperial County."

Hansen said, "Shit! Shit! Shit! Right in front of us all the time! Call NAF El Centro right now and advise them we think they'll be struck today by some type of terrorist attack and advise them we believe there are infiltrators in military and law enforcement uniforms."

It was that same venue in southeastern California where the Vintage B-25 "American Pride" was preparing for a special presentation at the 2021 El Centro Air Show. This was to be a first-of-its-kind demonstration of low level aerial bombing using the newly restored Norden Bombsight on the restored North American B-25 Mitchell. The plan as advertised to airshow attendees was to come in at low level over a paper target on the demonstration field, then drop four 500-pound practice bombs from their bomber. In coordination with prearranged pyrotechnics, it guaranteed quite a show for the crowd. The announcer and narrator would then describe how these bombers had first been used by General Jimmy

Doolittle off the USS Hornet at the beginning of WWII, then in brief detail how they had made the first strike against the Empire of Japan in the early days of 1942. The crew of the American Pride—Billy, Freddie, and Stevo—was drinking bottled water in the afternoon heat on the tarmac at NAF El Centro in the southwestern California desert near the Mexican border. Stevo said to Billy, "While you and Freddie finalize your flight plan, I'm going to finish up the electrical repairs." When Stevo was calibrating the Norden Bombsight, there had been some type of electrical malfunction causing the main bus breaker in the aircraft electrical system to flip, disabling the aircraft's electrical system entirely.

At around 1300 hrs., Billy and Freddie were talking through how their bomb run would go and Stevo was rapidly trying to repair the aircraft's electrical system. Billy and Freddie peered at the screen of their iPad10 with its advanced Google Earth Aviator's application—looking for any hazards to navigation and following their projected flight plan for the demonstration.

The demonstration flight was scheduled at 1430 hrs., shortly after a memorial service and missing man formation flown by the U.S. Navy's Blue Angels for the 20th anniversary of 9/11 had ended. While looking at the navigation charts on the iPad in the shade under the wing of the American Pride, the iPad went silent, as did the announcements by the show promoters and the sounds of aircraft engines on the tarmac. The crew's first thought was there was a massive power failure. Then they heard increased yelling by the spectators at the air show and realized some type of panic being generated.

Meanwhile, above the Naval Air Facility, the Blue Angels had just started their popular show for the crowd. Almost simultaneously, their F-18 Hornets' engines rapidly fell silent.

All five of the Navy F-18s then started to flounder and fall toward the ground. The crew watched as five canopies flew off along with five ejection rocket seats being pushed away from the aircraft in various directions. Being former jet fighter pilots, Billy and Freddie realized immediately there must have been a massive failure, because jet pilots are instinctively trained to punch out when specific situations arise. The three crewmen of American Pride looked around in alarm as Freddie wondered aloud, "What the fuck?"

The next five minutes stretched into what seemed more like 15, when the artillery shells started falling on the Naval Air Station, along with the sound of small arms fire in the air. The crowd started screaming, then began to scatter, running in all directions. As the crowd billowed out onto the taxiway, Billy said, "We've got to get out of here and now! Stevo, get the electrical back online ASAP!"

The Naval and Marine personnel at the air show had no immediate plan of action when the chaos erupted. With no communications equipment and no weapons, many took cover where they could find it. The Naval officers, Marine officers and senior NCOs started to take command as they had been trained. They organized small unit defensive positions, with minimum firepower and no way to immediately coordinate their efforts. Reverting to old proven training and experience, they immediately implemented runners between positions to coordinate their defense.

Navy Lieutenant Commander Andy Wood immediately looked for a way to get some weapons. Commander Wood was a former Navy Seal with expertise in small unit tactics. He spotted a Chief Petty Officer who was with the Naval Police Department, yelling and organizing his men into defensive positions. He called out to the CPO, "We need weapons, Chief. Get some of your men to the armory for whatever weapons they can find!" Chief Brockman nodded in acknowledgement and gave a thumbs up to the Commander.

"Chief, what's your name?" the Commander shouted out.

"Sir, Chief Petty Officer Edward Brockman," the CPO yelled back.

"Thanks, Chief. Be careful and be quick!" Commander Wood replied. Sizing up the situation, Commander Wood assumed the only weapons immediately available were the 9mm Beretta sidearms belonging to the military police personnel and Imperial County Sheriff's Deputies providing security at the event.

Military and civilian police officers across the base rapidly realized they needed to join the fight to defend the base and protect the panicked spectators. Those men jumped into their vehicles to head toward the gunfire but found their vehicles, along with their communications equipment, would not work. Many tried their cell phones and found them all without power.

As he had been asked, Chief Petty Officer Edward Brockman yelled to some of his men to get over to the armory and grab as many weapons and ammunition as they could carry. He then ordered them to take over to the defensive position established by Commander Wood.

Unknown to the CPO Brockman at the time, the armory safe door was closed with an electronic lock that was not now functioning. Instinctively, CPO Brockman then ran under fire over to a disabled police car. He grabbed at the shotgun in the electronic mount at the front of the unit. In frustration, he found it would not release without power from the battery being supplied to the electronic weapons lock. He saw a flash in front of the police car and looked up over the steering wheel. As if in slow motion, he saw the flash of a muzzle blast from a Marine Corps M-4 carbine leveled at him by a Marine Lance Corporal, which then raked the windshield on the squad car, killing him instantly.

Commander Wood saw Chief Brockman cut down trying to carry out his orders and yelled, "Fucking bastards!" Then, looking at the other sailors and Marines he had gathered up, yelled, "Look out gentlemen, we have infiltrators in American uniforms! Let's move over toward the second hangar and form a defensive position!"

As Stevo reconnected the electrical bus and the gages sprang to life, Freddie, cried out, "Let's get airborne and get the fuck out of here and maybe then we can figure out what the fuck is going on." Stevo ran over to an APU unit beside the B-25 and plugged it into the aircraft. Initially they were going to try an APU start to save the aircraft batteries. but found the auxiliary power unit would not even turn over.

"Shit!" yelled Billy. "Stevo, get in the aircraft; we will have to go with batteries." "Freddie, let's pray we don't have an issue with a battery start!" Slowly at first, then picking up speed, both engines started off the battery, belching out thick grey smoke from the engine exhausts. In a matter of minutes, the B-25 was taxiing away from the tarmac and trying to get through the crowd that was running out onto the taxiway trying to avoid being struck down by machine gun fire.

"Billy, the tower isn't responding to us on the radio and the cell is dead," Freddie reported. "In fact, we have no computer or satellite navigation."

"Shit, Freddie, we're on our own, let's operate VFR until we figure out what's happening," stated Billy. "Stevo, get in the nose and keep an eye out, buddy." He shouted over the drone of the B-25 engines reaching full power, "Well boys, I guess we'll know what the Doolittle boys felt like, because we're losing runway fast. Hold on."

Freddie was reading off the airspeed and conditions as they rolled down the runway with artillery blasts on either side. "Billy, repeating we have no navigation systems or GPS," he barked.

"What the fuck is going on?" whispered Billy to himself as the nose of American Pride cleared a six-foot-deep hole in the runway from an artillery burst by only a few feet.

As the B-25 American Pride banked to the left at the end of the runway with only about 200 feet of altitude, Stevo yelled out, "Fuck guys! There is infantry maybe a hundred or more pouring across from south of the base and they have ISIS flags on dozens of trucks, armored personnel carriers, Humvees, practice self-propelled guns and shit, and even about a half dozen tanks! They must be stolen; they're sporting markings of the Mexican Army," as bullets from a 50-caliber machine gun ripped through the nose glass of the B-25.

Almost in a state of shock, Stevo stuck his index finger through one of the holes, instinctively checking to see if it was real. Stevo thought to himself, "In all my time in the Corps and multiple deployments in harm's way, I've never had been shot at like this before."

"Billy, our communications equipment is not working!" shouted out Freddie. Muttering in desperation, he noted, "We have no FM radio, no navigation systems and no GPS. Fucking wonderful."

Stevo answered from the nose of the B-25, "Freddie, try the old AM set! I rebuilt that one. It was original in this type of plane in WWII. I haven't tested it yet, but I know it powers up!"

Billy looked at Freddie and shrugged his shoulders, "It's worth a shot. The Southern California CERT Teams operate off emergency AM amateur band radios. Maybe you can raise one? I know the City of Murrieta uses 1640 AM; let's start there."

Billy added, "They were doing a training scenario with the Riverside County Sheriff's Department last week at the airport and that's the frequency they were on. If you don't get anything after five to 10 minutes, start walking up through all the frequencies. I'm not sure what the others are. If you get a hold of them, have them get a hold of March Air Reserve Base. Tell them we are attempting to fly there with information on this situation."

"Mayday, mayday, mayday, this is B-25 American Pride calling on the blind on Emergency Frequency 1640 AM, over. Any station, any station, respond, over!" called Freddie in a calm and controlled voice. Only static returned on the radio.

"Freddie, keep trying the AM bands," Billy said. "God willing, we will pick up an amateur radio operator who is part of a CERT Unit."

"Mayday, mayday, mayday, this is B-25 American Pride calling on the blind on numerous emergency AM frequencies, over. Any station, any station, respond, over!" Freddie continued his way up the frequency list on the AM radio.

"Stevo, keep a lookout for other aircraft in the air or shit on the ground; we have no navigation systems!" Billy said. "Meanwhile, I guess it is dead reckoning to get us back home!"

Freddie, looking out his window, turned his head back to Billy and said, "Billy I don't know how much other air traffic we need to look out for. Look out my window at two o'clock low."

Billy looked over Freddie and saw the burning wreckage of a commercial Boeing 737 in a field and uttered, "Holy crap!"

In looking further, the landscape as far as they could see had thick plumes of black smoke rising into the air, which was very reminiscent to the fliers of the scene they'd witnessed during operation Desert Storm as the Iraqi Army left the oil fields of Kuwait burning. Freddie said in a soft voice, "Those are most likely other planes."

Billy, still looking at smoke in the distance, said, "Linda was flying to her folks in Pittsburg today." He paused for a moment and continued, "I never called her. I should have called her."

Consolingly, Freddie answered, "Easy buddy, stay the course. Let's get back and find out what happened, and we will locate her. Odds are she wasn't even in the air when this went down."

"Billy, there isn't even a thing moving on the freeway just stalled cars and what looks like wrecks," Freddie added, trying to change the subject.

Steve poked his head into the cockpit from the bomb bay area and said, "Holy shit, have you looked outside? There are people just standing on the freeway waving at us."

"Yes Stevo, we have," replied Freddie.

"What the hell happened, guys?" Steve asked.

"I don't know Steve. It's unreal," Freddie answered.

Billy spoke up and said, "EPW."

Both Freddie and Steve looked at him in with semi-bewildered expressions. "You know, an Electronic Pulse Weapon," Billy said. "That explains it all. The F-18s, loss of communications, no navigation systems, no radio, and what we see outside. We were lucky as shit that Steve was working on the electronic bus and had us completely powered down. That's why the APU wouldn't start and why we couldn't get the tower on the radio. God was watching out for us when we tried the battery start and we got out of there."

Billy wondered out loud, "We got hit and hit good today! We might be the only aircraft in the fucking country in the air right now! The equipment the ISIS troops hit us with must have been protected from the blast. What we need to do is get to March and hopefully land without their security shooting us down. We must report in to the Commanding General what we know, refuel somehow, and figure out some type of communications and armament, and head back for some recon near the border."

"What about Debbie, Freddie?" Billy suddenly asked.

It took Freddie a second to focus on the question, but he did answer. "She was supposed to be a home in Temecula with the kids. I didn't talk to her, either."

Billy turned back to Steve and started laying out instructions. "Think about the refueling thing and how we can arm this mother! Freddie, you keep trying the AM radio while I get us to Riverside."

After about 30 minutes of trying to make contact, a faint signal came over the old AM radio, "Unidentified aircraft calling, repeat, please repeat, over!"

Freddie answered, "This is B-25 American Pride we are en route to March ARB with emergency information for the commanding officer, over."

The voice on the other side replied, "This is Riverside County CERT. Do you know what has happened? It's pure panic here, over."

"Riverside CERT, I'm not sure, but if you can find a way to reach March ARB, tell them our ETA is about 25 minutes, over," Freddie answered back, but there was no reply. "Riverside County CERT, Riverside County CERT do you copy, over?" Freddie repeated over and over, hearing nothing but static back. "I hope they heard us," Freddie said, looking over to Billy, to which Billy just nodded yes.

Smoke was still drifting over NAF El Centro in the southeastern California desert. The ISIS troops had rounded up several prisoners, both civilian and military. Displaying the ruthlessness they are well known for, they murdered the wounded on the ground rather than dealing with them. Several hundred military members, law enforcement personnel, and spectators had escaped into the desert and scattered into several different directions. Commander Andy Wood had gathered some 50 military, law enforcement and civilians from the attack. The group moved into the desert, running, trying to get some distance between them and the invaders. Along the way, they managed to gather up several small arms, ammunition and some rations.

Wood wasn't sure what he was going to do, but it would be somewhere other than here, and somehow, they would have to become an effective resistance force and get in contact with U.S. military command. Unlucky residents of the area who were either too stunned, lost, or unable to keep up with those fleeing to the hills were gun downed without any mercy by the advancing enemy.

The ISIS military leaders had realized this, but they would deal with that threat later after their foothold in America had been established and the other parts of the plan unfolded throughout the U.S. These displaced Americans would not get far in the desert.

A military sedan pulled up in front of the NAS base headquarters and parked directly in front. Stepping out of the sedan was a Middle Eastern man dressed in pressed fatigues and wearing the rank of General in the Islamic States Army. Taking off his sunglasses was a man well versed in this operation, Haboob Wind. It was its author and implementer, Brigadier General Seem Abu Sheda. Quickly looking around, he said, "Make this my headquarters" to a lower ranking officer, who then saluted and walked toward the building.

A VERY DARK CLOUD DESCENDS

It was exactly an hour since the EPW attack had taken place in the atmosphere above the U.S. Iranian and North Korean scientists had determined the exact altitude for their weapons to detonate. This was critical, since North Korea had a limited number of ICBM delivery systems and Iran had a limited number of EPW weapons ready for deployment. They had determined that 10 weapons exploded at the proper altitude would allow the EPW to cover a specific area like a large cone and if the estimates were correct, should successfully cover at least 87 percent of the country.

The staged sleeper units would then wait and assess the situation, allowing for no longer than an hour to make sure all electronic equipment within their sectors was disabled. With that being determined, they would launch attacks on critical service areas around America, assuring they would remain useless after the American authorities and the American military began recovering disabled systems.

The effect on the general population of America immediately after the EPW blast varied from area to area, but an already frantic public had been shaken by the increase in lone wolf terror attacks. Initially, people were confused and frustrated when their ATMs would not work, or cell conversations were stopped in mid-sentence. The streets became clogged with motorists whose vehicles had stopped for no apparent reason. Traffic signals no longer worked, subways had stopped in mid-tunnel. To many people's horror, they witnessed sight of airplanes large and small falling from the sky and bursting into flames as they impacted the ground. The confusion then shifted to panic when the public realized no one was coming to help, nor could anyone even call for help. In some areas, vandalism, had started and looting of stores began to spread like a wildfire. Some individual police officers who were now on foot were powerless to stop the madness that was unfolding in front of them. Some people fell to the ground crying, some to their knees to pray, and a number had left their vehicles and began to run to their homes and loved ones. In medical centers from small to large, the scene was the same as power was lost during lifesaving surgeries and other procedures. Panic began to set in with even the seasoned medical teams when emergency generators did not activate seconds after the outages and even emergency flashlights would not work.

In some communities, local leaders realized there was an unprecedented situation unfolding before their eyes. In several larger and a few smaller communities, some antiquated communication systems were still being maintained and only vaguely mentioned in their emergency action protocols. Systems such as the obsolete fire alarm and police call box systems were still in place. Originally developed after the Civil War, they were a combination of Morse Code and a phone system added later in the 19th century. Initially run on a 6-volt battery system, over the years they were converted to a more advanced DC power system that ran off the commercial AC electrical grids. National guidelines required a redundant power system for these old systems, so in addition to the power of the electrical grids, there was an emergency generator backup system.

Several communities followed a recommendation for a third backup and maintained the battery system. In these communities, all police officers and fire engines had keys for these boxes. But as the years had progressed, many had no idea how to use this system, and had never opened one of the antiquated call boxes. When all the electronic devices stopped, the older precinct commanders realized they needed to implement an emergency communications system using those boxes.

Word spread through cities such as New York through runners and officers on bicycle who went to each district and advised command officers to have officers stand by the boxes, and then initiate an obsolete whistle code system for alerting other officers of emergency situations. It was also the only way the authorities could think of to continue to protect the public and respond to emergencies. It was situations like this that the sleepers would have to deal with after the initial EPW detonations to assist in neutralizing these agencies.

Unlike the defenders of America, the sleepers and invading terrorists had a limited system of communications. The American government might not be able to use the satellites in place, but the ISIS fighters were using protected satellite phones and a more limited range of military FM radios that were mainly to be used for local operations. What the invaders did have that was truly frightening were their "tacticals." These vehicles, protected from the blast, transported gunmen through communities throughout the country, shooting at random. There were relatively few of these, but to a panicked public, they provoked fear in citizens, law enforcement and military personal in the areas they were operating.

At 2:35 p.m., 65 minutes after the EPW detonations and the invasion into NAF El Centro, Lieutenant Alfred Washington stopped his Abrams Main Battle Tank, "Thunder 190," two miles east of the Fort Irwin area, approximately half a mile west of a major electrical power transformer hub and essential part of the California power grid. The terrorist crew of the tank began to fire several high explosive shells into the power station and high voltage towers. In less than 20 minutes, the sky around the area of the power station was filled with heavy black smoke from an extensive fire at the complex that would then spread to the brush in the area.

Lieutenant Washington then positioned his tank to watch over Fort Irwin Road, which connected the fort to Interstate 15, in case any type of relief force was sent. Through his binoculars, he could see another Abrams tank set up a mile to his east and another one to his west, also prepared to defend this road if need be. Three other tanks were taken in the pre-attack and they were to head over to the U.S. Army Bicycle Lake Army Air Field to watch for the possibility of any type of relief from the air.

At the Hoover Dam on the Colorado River in Northern Arizona, an hour and a half after the EPW detonation, a large explosion blew a hole into the mighty walls of the dam, creating a major break. The explosion was the result of another hijacked Abrams tank from the Arizona Army National Guard that had fired several HEAT rounds into the dam. The small hole it punched in the dam soon became a large crack traversing horizontally from the point of detonation in both directions for approximately 100 feet. Shortly thereafter, the ground around the Hoover Dam shook like a large earthquake. Within minutes, the base of the dam broke apart, with large portions of concrete falling to its base, followed by a tidal wave of water that had once been Lake Mead.

With the lack of any type of emergency communications, people living and enjoying what was to be a leisurely weekend on the Colorado River were hit with the horror of an unannounced wall of water cascading upon them—a tsunami of sorts that caused death and destruction from Laughlin, NV to as far as the Salton Sea in Southern California.

Whatever emergency services that could be gathered and allocated were now taxed well beyond their basic capabilities for what would be weeks. The dam breach would also render the hydroelectric plant within it to be permanently beyond repair, leaving a large portion of the Southwest without electricity. At the same time, this explosion was replicated at other hydroelectric dams, coal mines and wind farm power generating stations. Rendering these systems useless taxed emergency services across the country even further.

Along the Missouri and Mississippi rivers, explosions rocked the river locks that were maintained by the U.S. Army Corps of Engineers. This caused massive flooding from the heartland of America down to the Gulf of Mexico and left much of the river pathways useless for navigation. Similar events occurred across the U.S. with military precision. Aircraft that had fallen from the sky had started massive wildfires that would go on to rival the great Peshtigo Fire of 1871 in rural Wisconsin, which had been unstoppable and killed thousands of fleeing victims.

It was now 1750 hrs. in New York City as NYPD Officer David Williamson and his unit David 27A went back through his district and gave a situation report to his superiors via his SAT phone. People looked in amazement that he had a running vehicle and ran toward him, waving their arms and shouting. He had to speed through the areas because the crowds were filling the streets as their apartments were without power. Pulling onto an adjoining boulevard, he saw a uniformed officer standing next to a police call box that had its door open. Williamson reported to his superior that the NYPD has already assigned officers to the call boxes. He knew he would have to take out this box and others in the area—and his report would instigate an expedient destruction of others in the city. Officer Williamson parked about 25 feet away from the call box and took a military hand grenade from a satchel that was in the passenger seat next to him. As he walked up to the call box, the man standing next to it, who was from his precinct, yelled out to him, "Hey Dave, what the fuck is going on man? You still got a working squad!"

Just then, a terrorist tactical vehicle drove through the intersection firing randomly at anything that moved and continued down the adjacent street. "It's the end of days Jim!" Williamson responded, as he pulled out his service pistol and shot the other officer dead. Officer Williamson then holstered his pistol and was about to place the hand grenade into the call box. However, he was so focused he didn't see the two bicycle officers who observed him shoot the officer.

Officer Williamson stopped suddenly and turned around when he heard, "Halt Dave, drop your weapon!" He reached for the pin on the hand grenade, but both officers opened fire and Officer David Williamson dropped to the sidewalk with the hand grenade still clutched in his hand.

Meanwhile, all this didn't go unnoticed from an aerial platform that was the International Space Station. Astronauts on the space station could see the initial atmospheric blasts, 10 of them in all, which looked like small exploding clouds across America.

Initially, the astronauts were taken back trying to determine what they were. They had not seen the vapor trails of the North Korean ICBM missiles launched against America because they were over the far eastern Atlantic Ocean and their orbit had taken them over the eastern coast of the U.S. shortly after the last detonations had occurred. From space, they could observe the heavy smoke drifting across the country from California to North Carolina. They watched the unfolding flooding on the major American waterways. Realizing the situation below them to be a major incident, even possibly a nuclear attack, they began trying to contact NASA through various communication channels in addition to their computer systems.

After unsuccessful attempts to contact NASA through any system, some of the international astronauts attempted to contact their individual agencies via radio and computer communication lines as well, but to no avail. The reason for this was that all the International Space Station communications systems passed through the NASA nerve center in Houston. Houston was no longer functional, and neither were the satellites they relied on because they as well were routed through the Houston Space Center at NASA. It rapidly dawned on them that they were very much alone, with no way to contact the Earth.

It was almost 1600 hrs. on the west coast when the vintage B-25 American Pride began to bank over the north of March ARB and set up for landing. The large white M on the mountain north of the base was glowing brightly in the late afternoon California sun.

Billy, the pilot, was going over his landing checklist as he began to line up with the northern approach. The sound made by the landing gear was unusually loud for the crew of the bomber. Stevo was looking around the sky for any other aircraft that might be out there or any other hazards.

"Billy," Stevo blurted out as the plane banked, heading toward the runway, "look at Riverside, all the fires and no vehicles are moving on the streets, no fire engines, no cops. Look at the mall, people are looting everything in sight."

"Damn," said Billy. "But it looks like the base is secure at least for now."

Freddie, the copilot, was calling over the old AM radio into the blind announcing their intention to land at March ARB and which runway they would be coming in on. The crew was silent as the sound of the wheels hitting the main runway screeched and belched smoke after touching down. Looking out the windows of the aircraft, they could see the USAF security forces scattered around the runway and fence line armed with M-4 carbines and squad automatic weapons (SAWs). It was obvious the Air Force security personnel were overworked with frightened area residents trying to scale the base fences, fleeing an unknown enemy that had turned their world dark. Beside security personnel were bicycles they must have commandeered from the aircraft maintenance guys. As the B-25 taxied to the aircraft operations area, several of the bicycles with armed security personnel peddled alongside the American Pride and stood by as the B-25 shut down.

Upon exiting the aircraft, Billy handed his military ID card to a USAF Master Sergeant security officer. The sergeant saluted and said, "Sir, we heard you were en route and the CO is expecting you. Please follow us, sir." Following behind the security team, the crew looked over to the right and saw a government G550 parked near them and really thought nothing of it. It sat adjacent to the flight line next to a hangar and its doors were partially opened, looking like an impromptu command center containing little more than charts and maps. Walking toward the crew of the

American Pride was an Air Force Major General in an olive drab flight suit, holding his hand out in front of him.

"Gentlemen, I'm Major General Thomas Killdare. We got the message from a CERT volunteer who rode 10 miles here on a bicycle to tell us you were on the way. He said you had vital information, and God I hope so!"

"General, we're not sure, but we were under fire by enemy forces trying to get here from NAF El Centro, which was overrun by enemy infantry and armor," Billy told him. "Give me a map and we'll give you all our intel on what we went through, but I'm pretty sure we were hit with a EPW."

A man in a blue FBI T-shirt said, "EPW? I'm sorry, Supervisory Special Agent James Hansen, FBI Terrorism Task Force," came his late introduction.

Billy answered, "An Electronic Pulse Weapon at a minimum. Allow us to brief you and tell you of a plan we hatched on our way here." Billy and Freddie then went through the events of the day that had transpired some four or five hours earlier.

Stevo was out talking to the Air Force maintenance personnel, letting them know what they needed to do to prepare the American Pride for another flight as well as some thoughts he had for placing M-60 machine guns in several of its gun ports. From the maintenance hangar, he heard Billy yell for him to come over to the operations center. "General, this is retired USMC Gunnery Sergeant Steve McIntire, our resident B-25 expert and our third wheel, right Stevo?"

"Well, General, I had the main electrical buss disconnected when everything went down, and the explosions started," Stevo explained. "We were able to quickly get powered up and get out of there. As we were about 200, maybe 300 feet off the end of the runway, I saw about 100 infantrymen along with some light armor coming in from southeast of the NAS, and some of the vehicles were sporting ISIS black flags on what looked like Mexican Army vehicles. It looked like nothing was moving mechanical except for them, but I did see about 50 or so military personnel with small arms running north into the desert heading toward the Salton Sea as a group—one of them a Navy Commander who'd been looking at the B-25 prior to all this going down. I heard him yell out to some Marines and sailors to join up with him and form a defensive perimeter, but that was when we climbed into the B-25 and started to taxi out."

"It may have been him leading the group into the desert," Billy added, "but General, nothing was moving in the air or on the ground, at least what we could see. We saw numerous downed aircraft, including airliners with no emergency personnel helping. We also saw what appeared to be large-scale rioting here in Riverside General."

Hansen chimed in with, "Damn. We knew something was going to happen, but we didn't fathom this. It was only in the minutes before the attack we realized the target was most likely the El Centro NAS. We have a prisoner who we think is part of all this in the Conex next to the U.S. Customs office here one the base."

General Killdare, looking directly at Agent Hansen, voiced sternly, "Agent, we need more intel, and we needed it yesterday. Do what you have to do to get it!"

"But General?" Agent Hansen started, but was quickly interrupted by General Killdare.

"Agent Hansen, we don't even know if we have a country left," the General said. "Do I make myself clear? Do whatever you need to and now!"

"Yes, sir! But our prisoner may be more of a victim than a co-conspirator. We are still trying to ascertain that. I don't know how much more information he can give us," answered Agent Hansen. He nodded his head to Agent Grafton and motioned to the hangar door. They both exited the hangar, heading toward the Conex holding the prisoner.

Turning toward the crew of the American Pride, General Killdare said, "Gentlemen, I think he might be right on that. As of now, I am recalling you to active duty. Lieutenant Colonel Adams and Lieutenant Colonel Hoffman, you are promoted to the rank of Colonel. Gunnery Sergeant McIntire, I don't know if I can do this to a Marine, but I'm promoting you to a Master Sergeant in the Marine Corps, and if they ever have a problem with it, you can be Chief Master Sergeant in my Air Force any day!"

In unison, the three airmen snapped to attention, saluted, and said, "Yes, sir!"

General Killdare then said, "I want you to work with our maintenance crew and get your aircraft refueled and if possible armed, then proceed back toward the NAF El Centro area and do a reconnaissance of the situation. If possible, figure a way to contact whatever resistance is on the ground. In the meantime, get cleaned up, grab some chow and be back here in about an hour."

Newly promoted Colonel Hoffman and MSgt. McIntire walked toward the B-25 with the Air Force Maintenance Sergeant to discuss what could be done to get her ready. "General, I have a theory about reestablishing our communications," Billy said. "I believe from what I know about EPW is that any electrical equipment that is completely disabled and without any electrical power going to its circuitry might still be operational. I think we should get into the base exchange and see if we can locate any walkie talkies like the type they have for hunting, maybe even portable cameras such as GoPros. They will probably fire up if we put batteries in them. If so, General, then we can have some limited communications and possibly even be able to drop some radios to any resistance we have in the area."

General Killdare replied, "Colonel, take a couple of my security personnel. There are probably roving bands of thugs out there. Go find out."

REBIRTH

It was 20 minutes after eight in the evening at March Air Reserve Base. The base was completely dark on a moonless night, the only light coming from the glow of flashlights being held by the Air Force Security Police as they made rounds in pairs around the base perimeter. There was light radio traffic by the security personnel checking in with the command post using the two-way radios they had taken from the sporting good section of the Base Exchange. As theorized by Freddie, they were unaffected by the EPW blast earlier in the day.

The Air Force Civil Engineering Squadron was able to make a spare generator operational and it was providing limited power to the impromptu command center located in the maintenance hangar next to the tarmac by the B-25. Air Force maintenance crews were also able to set up a temporary fuel pumping system to refuel the American Pride for its early morning reconnaissance flight of the area around NAF El Centro.

Major Martinez called the flight crew over to a table he was standing next to. Billy and Freddie both looked up from the map that had helped them establish a timeline they would follow to, over, and back from the conflict area. The plan, if possible, was to make two low passes over the area, depending on resistance, and gather as much intelligence of the enemy's strength and positions as possible. Both walked over to Major Martinez, who threw back a tarp to reveal a variety of vintage CB radios. "One of our Com Flight sergeants worked at an electronic repair center and remembered they had a bunch of old CB radios in storage," Major Martinez said. "We rounded up batteries that would work with them, and a hand crank generator also taken from the air museum to provide power to the old vacuum tube base station. We now have some actual radio equipment."

General Killdare then spoke up. "I can tell by your expressions, gentlemen, and yes I can assure you they all work. What we came up with while you were gone is a plan if you should make contact any of our resistance forces."

Looking at General Killdare and his command staff, Billy said, "Fantastic, General. We know they have operational vehicles and as a result, recon capability. So, they're not going to stay put and you can't tell me they did all this to take over one naval air station." He added, "We have to assume there have been other breaches in our national security and at some point, and I'd say soon, they're going to hook up and move forward."

As Billy pointed at the map, he said, "We must see how far they have spread and with what. We have the portable radios from the Base Exchange along with this CB equipment, so if we locate any resistance personnel, we'll try to drop them and then attempt to establish communications with them. Then, we need to develop a strike plan and I'd say we need to implement it in no more than 48 hours to halt their movement."

General Killdare then said, "I'm sending two of our photography recon personnel with you. They have digital cameras that were still in the box at the Exchange, so they'll attempt to take photographic intel. What else do you need, Colonel?"

"General, I would say four more of your security personnel to man the defensive armament on the B-25," Billy said. "Tomorrow, I hope to have enough intelligence to form a retaliatory strike plan, but we have to move on this. I also made you a list of vintage flyable military aircraft in the area that were not at El Centro. If they are like the American Pride, they should be flyable. If we can get them here, hopefully within the next 24 hours, then jerry-rig some type of armament systems on them, we can have our strike force. In addition, you have a battalion here from the 75th Rangers and a platoon of a Marine Recon team scheduled to fly out next week, right?"

General Killdare nodded, "Yes, that's correct."

"Well, General, there are at least two vintage C-47 Skytrains and one C-53 Skytrooper right here in Riverside, and they've all have been used in vintage parachute drops by military airborne personnel," Billy stated. "If we get them here, we can send in a quick reaction force with whatever limited air support we can create from these warbirds. General, send one of the airborne officers to come with us and he can assess the situation at El Centro."

General Killdare looked at one of his operations officers and ordered, "Major, get on this ASAP. Some of the county CERT radios are back up on the amateur radio network running off generators. Maybe, just maybe, we can get word to these museums through them. Meanwhile, Colonel, why don't you and your crew get some rest? 0500 hrs. will come early and hopefully we'll have some other support aircraft here when you get back from your mission."

"General," Agent Hansen spoke up, "I'd like Agent Anderson to go with them tomorrow. He's an ex-Army Ranger and is top-notch on intel gathering."

"No problem," replied the general. "That's not a bad idea."

"Excuse me, General!" Billy cried, injecting himself into the discussion. "This is a military operation and not a law enforcement surveillance!" Looking directly at Agent Hansen, Colonel Adams added, "We don't have room for any of your people in that aircraft, and I don't see what purpose it would serve anyway."

"I don't want to invade your space colonel," Agent Hansen shot back, "but we have been chasing this down for years and Agent Anderson is one of the best in terrorist intelligence gathering. I know you are the aircraft commander, but damn it, I commanded an Army company in combat. This is a new enemy for both of us and the intelligence we may be able to gain can go on to assist you and others across the country when we finally can contact them!"

"Gentlemen, stop it right now!" General Killdare, said looking back and forth at both of them. "Last time I checked, I was the General and the guy in charge of all of this. We don't have time for bullshit turf wars; we don't have time for any of this crap! Colonel Adams, you will make room for Agent Hansen's man on your aircraft and give him your assistance within reason on this mission. Agent Hansen, advise your man that Colonel Adams is the aircraft and mission commander, so he is do as the Colonel commands while in the air."

There was silence for a moment as the men looked at each other and nodded. General Killdare sternly asked, "Is that clear gentlemen?"

Both replied, "Yes, sir," as the General dismissed them to get on with the mission preparation.

Agent Hansen turned to Agent Anderson. "Why don't you go get some sack time with the crew for tomorrow? Also, you heard that I'm sure, just be on your best behavior tomorrow; you were in the Army once and know what I mean, play the game," he said in a whisper with a little chuckle at the end.

With that, Agent Hansen walked back over to the General, where Billy and Freddie saluted, then turned and walked back out to the B-25 accompanied by Agent Anderson to find Stevo, so they could all go get some rest before the early morning mission. "Colonel, no worries on me. I won't get in the way and I'll follow your orders to the letter on the mission," Agent Anderson told Billy.

"Damn straight, I know you will, Agent," Billy replied with all the authority you would expect of a military leader.

As the three airmen and FBI agent stood by their aircraft, a pair of headlights came onto the tarmac heading toward the hangar and the command center. "What the fuck?" Freddie blurted out while security personnel surrounded the entrance to the command center with automatic weapons at the ready. Coming to a halt was a military Humvee with an Air Force Captain jumping out and running toward the hangar, yelling, "General! General Killdare!"

General Killdare came out of the hangar and stopped suddenly as the Captain came to attention and saluted. General Killdare returned the salute and asked the obvious, "Captain, where in the hell did you find a running Humvee?"

"Sir," replied the Captain. "The mechanics at the motor pool had this Humvee in for service and it was partially disabled. They put it back together by flashlight and it started up, sir."

The General looked at the three airmen and said, "If this one runs, there are probably others out there. If we discovered it, I'm sure the enemy will know it is possible and they will make a target of any services we might be able to return to operation: power plants, communications centers, and so on. Tomorrow's mission takes on even more importance!" General Killdare made his point while shaking his head back and forth.

It was 4:30 in the morning on Sunday, September 12, 2021 and the sun hadn't even begun to peek over the Palm Springs mountains. The Humvee pulled up in front of the crew rest building to pick up the three airmen along with FBI Agent Anderson. Major Martinez was driving, and he gave a couple of honks on the horn of the Humvee. The four, accompanied by frequent yawns, slowly got into the Humvee, with Billy taking the passenger seat next to the driver. "Good morning, Major," Billy said.

"Good morning, Colonel," Martinez replied.

It was only about a six- or seven-minute drive to the flight line, where their B-25 was waiting for their preflight. Rounding the corner of the hangar that was now housing the impromptu command center, a bright glow highlighted the corner of the building. Stevo blurted out, "Holy Shit!" Before anyone else could speak up, they saw the glow of field maintenance lights that had illuminated the B-25 from all angles.

Major Martinez informed them, "Our Civil Engineer Flight got another generator working and hooked up the maintenance lights. They were up most of the night. Well, at least until 0200

hours, making sure they were all up for our CAM mechanics."
"CAM?" questioned Agent Anderson.

"It's our Consolidated Aircraft Maintenance Flight. Our Com Flight will be here also for a briefing. Agent, that is Communications Flight," the Major added with a chuckle.

Walking up to the B-25, the four looked at five eight- by four-foot banquet tables that held a variety of small arms, food, and the CB radio equipment—all in bundles with modified parachutes attached to them. Standing by the table was General Killdare, Agent Hansen and Agent Grafton. "Good morning, gentlemen," General Killdare said as he greeted the crewmen.

Freddie said, "Someone has been pretty busy overnight."

Before there was a reply, Stevo came back from the B-25 and said, "She is beautiful, and with 50-caliber machine guns, not the M-60s we talked about last night."

"Last night we went over to the 138th Armored Cavalry Regiment of the California Army National Guard in Riverside. Their vehicles are not running, but their machine guns don't run off any electricity. So, we borrowed a few," Major Martinez said.

General Killdare added, "We then did what the Air Force has been doing for the past five years or so. We sent some mechanics over to the March Field Air Museum and took the mounts off its B-25 and used them on yours. We didn't put any in the upper turret. We are not figuring you will have issues with any aerial threats."

Slowly, out of the shadows, came two U.S. Army Rangers who had been waiting along with their battalion at March ARB to ship out the following week. The General motioned over two soldiers to make introductions. "Sergeant Fillmore and Specialist Shaw, this is Colonel Adams and Colonel Hoffman. They are the aircraft commanders and will be overseeing this operation."

Both Rangers replied, "Sirs," and Colonel Adams and Colonel Hoffman nodded to acknowledge them.

General Killdare then briefed the flight crew on the overnight changes to the reconnaissance plan. "Gentlemen, in addition to doing a reconnaissance of the area, you are to attempt to visually contact any remaining ground resistance forces that might have escaped. Our intelligence officers have identified these three locations around the southern Salton Sea area that could provide some cover for our troops. According to the information you provided Colonel Adams, they were last seen heading in that direction. Make sure you check for stragglers in those areas. They are highlighted on the map."

He went on, "Next, if located, attempt to contact them. When contact is established, these two Rangers will make a low-level drop from your aircraft out of the bomb bay. They will let you know what they need after this briefing. They will take the radio equipment and set up a communications outpost and distribute the portable radios to the resistance fighters. After that has been accomplished, I want you to drop these small arms, ammunition, MREs, radios, and medical equipment to them." The General asked for clarification, "You all understand how important this is?"

All three airmen agreed, "Yes, sir!"

"Good!" General Killdare said. "When we make our assault, they will be essential for communications and ground coordination."

Looking at Major Martinez, General Killdare gave further direction, "Major, take over."

"Oh, one more thing," the General added. "Damn, I'm tired. We got messages out to all the museums you wanted to contact, and a list of what you we're looking for. We don't have any word back yet, but we did get a confirmation through the CERT radio system that the messages were delivered."

Major Martinez then took over, telling the crew how overnight the Com Flight had installed a CB radio into the aircraft and all radios would be set to channel 23. He also explained there would be several alternate channels in the event of any type of interference. After Major Martinez finished, the two Army Rangers explained to the crew that they were setting up a system to drop the equipment and supplies with modified parachutes. They then showed Stevo how to drop them out of the bomb bay after they had left the aircraft and established a drop zone.

Agent Hansen walked over to Agent Anderson, who was standing next to the flight crew and told him, "Bill, you are just an extra set of eyes. Just see what you can help these intel guys with and be careful." Agent Anderson nodded his head and reached out to shake Agent Hansen's hand, saying, "I will, Jim. Thank you."

With that, Agent Hansen turned and walked back toward the Conex and the prisoner.

Major Martinez informed the crew, "We also have a CERT radio set up here in operations and it will operate on this frequency with you." He then motioned to a gentleman sitting at a radio set in the command center, "Tony, come over here please." The gentleman stood up and came over to the group and Major Martinez continued, "This here is Tony Wallis. He is the head of Riverside County CERT and he will be running their communications from here and will be your radio contact with the command center."

"Tony here is also an ex-Army paratrooper with the 101st Airborne during Desert Storm. In addition, he is a retired Battalion Chief from the Los Angeles City Fire Department. So, he is well suited for this," General Killdare added.

Tony gave the crew a breakdown on the communications setup on the aircraft and an addition to the original AM radio on the B-25. "Gentlemen, the CB radios are good for maybe up to a couple of miles or line of sight communications. In fact, they will be perfect for air-to-air communications between the aircraft. However, to reach back here to the command center, we'll have to use the aircraft's old AM radio. We have installed the original Morse Code key in the aircraft and have one here at the command center. I'm sending one of our CERT guys with you to man the AM radio who is well versed in Morse Code from the Boy Scouts. We also have a vintage AM radio from the museum with a hand crank generator for the Rangers to contact us from the ground with Morse Code. I'll man the AM radio on this end. We used it as a backup communication in the Army in Desert Storm."

Colonel Adams confirmed what he heard. "Okay, roger that, Chief!" With that, the three airmen began their historic preflight of the American Pride for its first combat mission in over 80 years. It was now 0600 hrs. and the breaking sunlight was beginning to come up over the top of the mountains that separate Riverside from Palm Springs. Billy took a small photo of his wife Linda out of his flight jacket, kissed it and placed it on the instrument panel of the bomber. Freddie watched him and then said in a broken voice, "My only pictures are on my phone."

The B-25 taxied to the end of the runway and started powering up the engines, picking up speed as it proceeded down the runway. Lifting off, the B-25 did a gentle bank to the left and headed south toward the Salton Sea area.

As Agent Hansen approached the Conex, Agent Grafton, who was sitting at the door, rose to meet him. "Sue, let's try this again," he said, and they both entered the Conex. Agent Hansen took a chair and placed it at the table directly across from Deputy Butterfield. "Good morning Deputy," Agent Hansen said to open the conversation.

"Did you get any word back about my family?" Deputy Butterfield asked.

"Yes, they are fine." After a few seconds of silence, Agent Hansen continued. "But you knew that, didn't you?" Deputy Butterfield was silent and just stared at Agent Hansen. "Do you know you were a dead man deputy?" Hansen asked.

"What do you mean?" Deputy Butterfield responded slowly.

"We have been following these incidents for a while and one thing has always been consistent. Do you know what that one thing is?" Agent Hansen asked. There was no response from the prisoner, so Hansen continued. "There has always been one local law enforcement officer involved, and that officer always ended up dead in the end. And guess what? I do believe the officer this time was you, deputy."

After a few moments of silence, Deputy Butterfield spread his hands out above his head and said, "Praise be to God!" He then slowly clapped his hands and said, "Very good, agent. Our sacrifices will be rewarded in Heaven. I'd now like my lawyer."

Agent Hansen looked over toward Agent Grafton, laughed and then clapped his hands. Looking back at Deputy Butterfield, he said, "You don't get shit!"

As Deputy Butterfield looked confused, Agent Hansen looked at Agent Grafton and said, "Agent, why don't you tell the deputy why he won't get shit?"

Stepping next to Agent Hansen, Agent Grafton said, "That is because we are at war and this is not a law enforcement operation. This is a military one and to me you look like a spy."

With that, both agents headed toward the door. Agent Hansen turned and said, "Thank you, deputy. You gave us more information from your inaction than if you would have talked to us. Enjoy Heaven."

❖ ❖ ❖

A half an hour into the mission, the early morning sun caused a massive reflection to the east. As the American Pride drew closer to the area, the crew observed massive flooding, which now had increased the size of the Salton Sea by nearly 50 percent.

"Shit, where did all that water come from?" Billy asked on the aircraft intercom.

"Sir, one reason I can think of is that the Hoover Dam has been taken out," replied FBI Agent Anderson.

Billy instructed the CERT operator to report back to the March ARB Command Center via the AM radio frequency. He then addressed the entire crew by intercom, "If they took out the

Hoover Dam, then I'm guessing they also took out other power generation centers along with any other services they think we may able to repair. Keep your eyes out for anything else like this. Stevo, keep your eyes open in the nose for anything else we need to advise March about."

The B-25 made its way south above the Salton Sea, looking for the new southern shoreline. Upon seeing it, Billy decreased their altitude to 1,000 feet and instructed the crew to look for any survivors. The new shoreline was now approximately two miles north of El Centro.

Since the Salton Sea was so close to El Centro now, Billy had decided to go directly over the NAF El Centro for the reconnaissance, then look for the survivors. The left waist gunner's voice came on the intercom, "Sir, I just saw a reflection coming from the east; it could be a rescue mirror." Freddie responded on the intercom, "Billy, that is the North Algodones Dunes area. They probably headed over there because of the flooding."

"Roger that, let's check it out," Billy replied while banking the B-25 to the left.

After leveling out, Billy advised the crew they were only about 10 minutes from the area and to keep their eyes open. Billy no sooner released the talk button on the intercom when tracers raced past the B-25's cockpit, striking the right side of the fuselage, hitting FBI Agent Anderson with shrapnel and rendering him unconscious. The right waist gunner returned fire on what looked to be two desert-colored Humvees with 50-caliber machine gun roof turrets. The American Pride's waist gun cut through the Humvees like a hot knife on soft butter, with the final blow coming from the rounds fired from the B-25's tail gun.

As the pair of Humvee's burst into flames that reached high into the air, Billy got on the intercom, requesting a status update. He was advised of some minor damage and informed that Agent Anderson had been hit and was unconscious. One of the Air Force photographers was providing first aid to him and he appeared to be stable.

Billy looked at Freddie and said, "They had a patrol out looking for the survivors, so I think we're in the right place."

Just then, Stevo called out from the nose, "We got them about 11 o'clock. Maybe 50 guys, two of them are holding up an American flag up between them." Billy then rocked his wings in acknowledgement of seeing them on the ground. Banking back around, the bomb bay doors opened slowly on the B-25 as a small parachute attached to a package fell out, containing a portable radio along with some water and MREs.

Within a few minutes, the radio crackled with, "Calling unidentified American Aircraft, over." With that, the reconnaissance crew on the B-25 American Pride had made radio contact with the survivors of the El Centro attack. Billy told them they would be dropping two personnel and several packages of equipment for them. Billy began his ascent up to 5,000 feet so the two Army Rangers could make their jump down to their fellow Americans.

After dropping the equipment packages, Billy advised the Rangers that they were continuing with their recon mission and to do their check-in with the command center at March for further instructions. As the B-25 banked toward NAF El Centro, the pilots could hear the tones of Morse Code being tapped out to the March Command Center from the Rangers for a radio check. When March tapped a message back to the Rangers, a sigh of relief came from Billy.

AFTERNOON OF DISCOVERY

After leaving the Rangers and survivors on the ground, Billy banked the B-25 to the east with the plan of doing reconnaissance over the Naval Air Station from that direction, out of the sun, hoping it would give them a little extra protection. Billy directed the CERT radioman to contact March for a communications check and advise they would be starting the reconnaissance pass in about 10 minutes.

Billy dropped the B-25 down to about 1,000 feet and advised the crew, "Get ready, we're going in; gunners keep watch, intelligence guys get ready. Stevo, keep an eye on as much as you can from the nose; only call out if it is important, pilot out."

Almost immediately, the B-25 was buffeted by explosions near the aircraft from ground fire. Stevo called out, "We have one, two mobile radar units working, and it looks like some truck-mounted anti-aircraft guns on both sides of the runway."

Billy responded, "Roger that, gunners see what you can do about those AA trucks. This place is hot, so this will be our only pass."

With that, Stevo started raking the field in front of the aircraft with his 50-caliber machine gun, while both waist gunners raked each side of the aircraft on the ground and the tail gunner finished what they had missed on the way past each burning vehicle. The minutes dragged on intensely. The B-25 flew past the air station's control tower with the tail gunner firing his twin 50-caliber machine guns into it on the way out of the air station. Billy banked the B-25 to the north, heading back toward March Field while climbing to about 10,000 feet when the right engine started to sputter and spew black smoke. Looking at Freddie, Billy said, "Freddie, feather number one 1."

"Roger that," Freddie replied.

Billy then got on the intercom. "Status report, wounded and damage?" The reports came back that no one other than Agent Anderson had been wounded and there were a few holes, but nothing serious. Billy then told the CERT radioman to contact March Command Center and advise them they were on the way back with one wounded and right engine damage.

The B-25 was now 20 minutes out of landing at March Air Reserve base. It was around 1430 hrs. and the crew was exhausted from the long mission. They had radioed ahead with the CB radio, requesting to have a medical team waiting to handle the wounded officer and maintenance ready to look at the damaged engine.

Once again, the large white M on the mountaintop came into view as the B-25 began to descend for landing. On its final approach, Stevo called out from the nose of the aircraft, "Hey guys, will you look at that?" To their left, over by the base control tower, was a line of vintage aircraft that had been brought in from the other flying museums in Southern California. As they taxied over toward the command center hangar, they could see General Killdare, Major Martinez and Agent Hansen all standing. While the base medical personnel tended to the wounded officer, Colonel Adams, Colonel Hoffman, and MSgt. McIntire walked with the trio into the command center.

"Great job, gentlemen, on a rough assignment," General Killdare said. "We've made some advancements here; some you can see and some you can't. First, the obvious. We have the aircraft here you requested and our CAM personnel have been working nonstop since they got here to arm them and prepare them for a strike tomorrow morning. And, they solved the refueling problem by taking manual hand pumps from the museum and attaching them to our fuel supply lines."

"Tomorrow?" Billy repeated.

"Yes Colonel. Tomorrow morning," the General replied, redirecting his gaze to Agent Hansen. "Agents Hansen and Grafton were unable to gather any more information from our prisoner while you were gone. But he did finally confirm he was part of all this, and from what he told us previously and what we found in his SUV along with the storage locker, we were able to piece some things together."

Agent Hansen, looking at Billy, said almost tauntingly, "Colonel, with your permission I want to show you this."

General Killdare quickly said, "Agent!"

"Sorry, sir," Agent Hansen said while he spread out a map of the El Centro area. "We believe NAF El Centro was the step-off location for this invasion of the continental U.S. He said he didn't know why they had picked it specifically, but we theorized that the area south of the border held several areas where they could hide assets. It was also the only military installation near the border that had an air show scheduled on September 11 and security would be lax.

"There was a new radical Jihad army that morphed out of ISIS," he continued. "They started planning this shortly after our pullout of Iraq. While we focused on ISIS and its affiliates, this army grew in the shadows with a plan to work together on a major assault on the U.S. scheduled for the 20th anniversary of the September 11 attacks. This deputy immigrated to the U.S. as a child from Yemen. He keeps saying he was forced to do what he did because his family was being held, but I really feel he and others were to infiltrate within our public safety, intelligence, and military organizations with the one focus of this invasion.

"We believe he was actually one of the leaders here in America," Agent Hansen went on, "and the plan was to use the Naval Air Facility in El Centro as its headquarters, to funnel men and machinery through there. Other sleeper groups using stolen and captured equipment could then take control of predetermined locations in America. We found other data from a laptop at the storage locker. Their plan, called Haboob Wind, would spread across America from the Southwest until we were defeated. So, their headquarters is at El Centro and this operation is under the command of General Seem Abu Sheda, who also happens to be the mastermind of the entire plan.

"One other thing," Agent Hansen added. "Sheda was one of our translators and local contacts in Baghdad. I worked with him directly, especially on our departure. I always thought he was a friend. That's the way I remember him—friendly, helpful and one of the good guys. I guess we were all fooled by him, as he was actually a general in this new radical army."

General Killdare then took over the briefing. "Colonel Adams, it was an EPW weapon, only not like one we ever anticipated. We also made contact through other CERT communications operators and some amateur radio operators running off generators. We are starting to establish some type of communications grid. It is unsecured at this time, but Tony is running the net and we have contacted NORAD at Cheyenne Mountain, which are running off its own EP-shielded generators. Hopefully, we will be back with some reliable normal communications with the upper echelons. However, what we have pieced together is that while we thought we were monitoring Iran's nuclear program and keeping it in check, they were creating and perfecting an EPW weapon system for this jihadist army. They then worked with North Korea and its ICBM system, the very one we mocked for years, to deliver the weapons over America. How they got through our early detection systems, God only knows, but we assume it was with the assistance of other sleepers.

"We notified NORAD about the sleepers," he continued, "and they told us security forces had shot and killed a Colonel who worked in the early warning center as he tried to set satchel charges around their emergency generators prior to the attack. Apparently, he was trying to ensure that NORAD would be dark also. We also have heard from other emergency command centers through the CERT net of mass panic and rioting, so this is bad all over this country, just as this group had hoped for.

"So, gentlemen, now as for why tomorrow?" General Killdare forged ahead. "Their own timetable shows they plan on being in and taking over Washington, D.C. in 7 to 10 days. That is 7 to 10 days from now. So, we can't wait. We just can't. We need to cut off the head of the snake and kill it, then gather whatever other intel we can from their headquarters. We're getting word the best we can to other commands as to tomorrow's operation.

General Killdare looked stoic, paused, then added, "Get cleaned up and some chow in you. We'll have a briefing with you and the other flight crews on your mission for tomorrow at 1800 hrs."

General Killdare then took Colonel Adams and Colonel Hoffman off to the side and told them, "Gentlemen, I'm so sorry, but we still don't have any word on your family's status. We're trying, but with our limited communications ability it's taking time. But I swear to you we will get you some answers."

"Thank you," Billy replied, adding, "Colonel Hoffman and I appreciate all the efforts, General."

"Yes, General thank you," Freddie added to the conversation, before both officers saluted the General and walked away.

As the three airmen were leaving, Agent Hansen asked if he could ride with them back to their quarters before they went for chow.

"Colonel Adams, I want to let you know that I know you are the commander of this mission,"Hansen said. "I respect that, and I apologize for my taunting earlier. Now, I want to ask permission for Agent Grafton and me to go in with the Rangers and Marines tomorrow."

"And why should I allow this, Agent Hansen?" Billy asked.

"Colonel, I know Sheda, I know what he looks like," Agent Hansen replied. "As for Agent Grafton, she is one of the best analysts on the team. Plus, when she was in the service, she had an airborne rating and I believe has had some flight training."

"So, do you want some payback?" Billy asked.

"Hell yes, I do," Agent Hansen nodded, "but more than that, I can identify him and make sure we get the right guy and Agent Grafton knows what intelligence we need to grab first—and yeah, I also want payback."

"That's good enough for me," Billy replied. "We will see you two at the briefing. I want to apologize also; I'm originally a fighter jock and we like being loners. I guess my nose was a little out of joint."

With that, Agent Hansen headed over to the Conex where DART had been working out of. Walking in the office, he grabbed two cups of coffee and sat down at the desk where Agent Grafton was going over maps of the El Centro area. "What's up Jim?" she said, looking up.

He got straight to the point. "Sue, we're going on the mission to retake El Centro tomorrow and hopefully capture Sheda. I want you to go with us. You're the best agent on the team and I really need your intelligence expertise." Then with a chuckle, he added, "you've also jumped from a perfectly good airplane before."

"Okay, Jim, I'm ready if you need me. You know you can always count on me," Agent Grafton said while taking a sip of coffee, holding the cup with both hands.

"Great," Agent Hansen said while standing up and heading to the door. "I'll see you at the briefing." Then, walking outside, he thought to himself, "Damn it, Jim, you had a chance to say something and didn't."

❖ ❖ ❖

The three airmen along with the two FBI agents arrived at the briefing room about 20 minutes early. While walking past the aircraft on the flight line, they saw the base CAM personnel still working on placing weapons back onto the vintage planes. To start the briefing, Major Martinez stood in front of a large map of the El Centro Naval Air Station and surrounding areas. In explaining the early morning mission to the variety of vintage military aircraft pilots and their crewmembers, he stressed the importance of what they were about to do. There would be minimal bombing and the B-17s would only be used if enemy forces were to head out en masse from the strike area. Each aircraft only has a few rapidly modified bombs if needed and nothing for a sustained bombing campaign.

Major Martinez further explained that with communications established with the survivors of the El Centro attack, they would infiltrate the air station and eliminate any potential early warning systems the invaders may have put into place. Billy and Freddie's B-25 would be the aerial command center over the target area and all coordination between the command center, ground assets, and aerial assets would go through it. The Army Rangers and Marines would go in with a low level dropout from the vintage paratroop transports. All other aircraft would provide close air support for the ground forces. It was necessary to make sure the enemy command and control centers were neutralized and if possible, any ranking personnel be captured for interrogation, specifically General Sheda. FBI Agents Hansen and Grafton would be going in with the Rangers' 3rd Platoon so they can locate, identify and hopefully capture him. The final part of the plan was to neutralize their command and control center.

The hanger filled with the hastily assembled fight crews sat waiting for a briefing on the mission they would be flying with their vintage aircraft. The room grew silent with the sight of General Killdare approaching in his military dress uniform.

Major Martinez yelled out, "Attention" as the General approached the podium and the seated crews all stood up from their chairs.

General Killdare motioned with a downward movement of his hand as he said, "At ease, please." The crews retook their seats as he began to speak.

"Pilots and crews," he said. "I just want to say a few words before Major Martinez continues with the mission briefing. You are all patriots! You are the best of what makes us Americans. Today, you will be battling to repel an invading force upon our land; not since 1812 have we had an enemy army invade the continental boundaries of our great nation. You are the tip of our spear, the patriots who will show that we will not go away without a fight. This is our Lexington, this is our Concord; the very essence of our democracy is at stake and on your shoulders. Some of you are veterans and those who have combat experience need to teach those who have never worn the uniform. For you who have never seen combat, learn from those who have. We don't know what's happening in the rest of the country currently, but we know what's happening right here and right now. Your victory today will ring across this vast nation louder and faster than any of our old communication systems could have. Today, patriots, today is your day. Today is America's day! Major Martinez, please go ahead with your briefing."

As Major Martinez approached the podium, General Killdare motioned to him to hold up. General Killdare looked back at the flight crews and said, "I'm sorry, Major, one more thing and I'll be done. Patriots, I don't know how to stress anymore what tomorrow means for all of us and our country's future. If we don't succeed tomorrow, I'm truly afraid that our days as a nation are numbered. We can't fail; we won't fail." Finally, the General said, "When your briefing has concluded, make sure everything is ready for tomorrow, eat a good meal and get some rest. We'll see you here tomorrow at 0430 hrs. for a final briefing before departure."

With that, Major Martinez walked up to the lectern, saluted General Killdare and went on with his briefing.

After the briefing, Agent Hansen and Agent Grafton walked back to the Conex they had been using as an office. Agent Hansen pulled up a chair and sat down at Agent Grafton's desk, next to her, saying, "Sue, I have to say something before tomorrow."

"Sure, Jim. What's up?" Agent Grafton replied, looking squarely at his eyes.

"I was going to head over for some chow," Hansen answered, "and I want to see if want to join me."

"I was going to head over later because I'm really busy getting things ready here for tomorrow," she said, looking concerned that something was wrong, "but if you want me to come with you now, I will."

"Okay, this is it, Sue," Agent Hansen said in a soft and almost apologetic tone. "For years, I wanted to ask you to dinner and I always held back because I was your boss. I don't know what to say, but I have a feeling if I don't ask you now, it might never happen."

Looking back at Agent Hansen, Agent Grafton put down her pen and said, "So soldier, you are saying with the mission tomorrow, we might not come back, so I better finally ask her?" Agent Hansen looked surprised as she continued. "I've waited a long time for you to ask, I've dropped you enough hints, now let's go eat. And when we get back, I expect a decent dinner and not this military chow."

With a big grin, Agent Hansen replied, "Yes, of course, oh wow!"

Agents Hansen and Grafton headed out of the Conex toward the makeshift dining facility, chatting and laughing.

NEW AGAIN

It was 0600 on September 16, 2021, five days after the invasion of America. The desert between Arizona and California was awash with a rainbow of colors all too familiar to those who live in the Southwest. Looking out the cockpit window of the lead aircraft of the "New Air Commandos," Colonel William "Billy" Adams USAF saw his ragtag strike force. Billy chose the name from the famed Army Air Force unit that had fought in the Burma-India Theater in World War II. They were a combined unit of aircraft and specialized ground personnel doing things they were never trained for and succeeding. He had always admired that air unit, so he took its name and reactivated it for their mission. As a nod to nostalgia, Billy also had the white striping that had identified the original Air Commandos put on their aircraft fuselages. It was a beautiful sight, these vintage aircraft heading out once again to defend America, many of which had not flown in combat since WWII or the Korean War. It was hard to believe that in the matter of a few days, he and his crew went from planning to show their restored North American B-25 Mitchell Bomber at air shows to being recalled to active duty, promoted, and leading a vintage strike force from America's past.

Billy kissed his index finger and touched the picture of his wife Linda on the instrument panel, saying softly, "I love you baby," while reflecting on the past few days.

After convincing the commanding general at March ARB to follow his plan, Billy and his crew organized the collection of restored and airworthy museum aircraft from the Southern California area. With the help of the maintenance personnel from the Air Force at March ARB and the various museums, these aircraft had new weapon systems restored to them. The crews worked tirelessly to restore some weapons, mainly the 50-caliber machine guns in the fighters, and outfit the bombers with a combination of the more modern M-60 caliber machine guns and a few remaining 50-caliber weapons. In addition, the bomb bay areas of the bombers were restored to the point that they could hold and drop an array of actual aerial ordinance and even some makeshift aerial bombs. All the crews had never flown combat with vintage aircraft, so classes were held using vintage manuals from the March Field Air Museum as the base for learning tactics and strategies of WWII aerial combat. There would be no time for practice, so the first time would have to go flawless.

Looking from side to side, Billy saw five other B-25 Mitchell Bombers, two B-17 Flying Fortress Bombers, two A-26 Invader Attack/Bombers, four P-51 Mustang Fighters, two P-38 Lighting Fighters, two P-47 Thunderbolt Fighters, and two P-40 Tomahawk Fighters. Also in this squadron were three vintage transport aircraft: two Dakota C-47 Skytrains and a C-53 Skytrooper. As they did during WWII, they were carrying Army and Marine Corps recon paratroopers—70 of them today.

Many of these airborne troopers had made demonstration drops from these aircraft at airshows in the past, so they were somewhat familiar with the type of jump they would be making. The difference this time? It would be under live fire. A lot of ingenuity, sweat and effort had gone into creating this initial response to the invasion that had taken place a mere five days earlier. The attack plan was simple. The bombers would be used to soften the drop zone area for the paratroopers. After the drop, they would gather aerial intel if possible of the area. The troopers would land in the designated drop zone and link up with the resistance forces that were in the area after the initial attack and under the command of Navy Commander Andy Wood. The fighter aircraft and A-26 Assault/Bombers would provide close air support for the paratroopers as they proceeded to retake the El Centro Naval Air Station, crush the opposition, and capture the leadership if possible.

The mission planners had made a calculated assumption that the invaders were faced with some of the same problems they were— mainly having limited communications due to the restrictions of the line of sight communications and the limited range of the portable CB radios given to the survivors and being used by the Army Rangers and Marines. The invaders also had portable military radios that were more advanced than the CB radios, but had a limited effective range of less than 10 miles. The enemy had the advantage of operating vehicles and it was hoped that some of these could be captured by the Rangers and Marines. One of the advantages the Americans did have is that the improvised CERT communications system had allowed the military and civilian authorities to re-establish a rudimentary communications grid.

The U.S. was not totally blind, as the invaders had hoped they would be. The American military would not likely have access to radar or satellite intelligence for a while, but by reverting to reconnaissance techniques perfected in World War II, they were adapting to the challenge and responding. So, the thought was that this strike force would most likely be undetected until it got close enough to the air station for invader's scouts or radar to spot them.

One of the first elements of the attack was to have the survivors take out these sites prior to the arrival of the strike force. They also figured the chance of any type of aerial confrontation might be nonexistent or minimal.

Looking at his watch and seeing that it was 0638 hrs., Billy ran a communications check with the other aircraft on their CB radios. He then announced, "Twenty minutes till target, radio silence until then, and keep your eyes open, no need to acknowledge!" With the completion of the transmissions, all the flight crews checked their equipment. Stevo and the other bombardiers double-checked their Norden bomb sights in case they were needed and then waited. Billy also instructed the CERT radioman to contact the March Command Center with the information.

In the early hours of the morning, small squads of the resistance force moved into place, quietly, between the enemy patrols and outposts. They set up on known enemy scout outposts and waited. Two other squads closed in on the two mobile radar units the reconnaissance had discovered yesterday. These were the first objectives the resistance forces had reached—and they needed to be taken out before the Air Commandos were detected. In addition to the radar stations, the resistance squads also covered any means of entrance or exit to the air station to prevent any retreat or reinforcements from the area. They successfully neutralized the radar units in the hour before the attack commenced. It was estimated that the arrival of aircraft and paratroopers would be between 0705 and 0715 hrs. PST. They would be notified by a series of beeps over the portable CB radios within five minutes of the strike force's arrival. At that time, they would neutralize their objectives and prepare to defend the points of entry onto the base.

The tones had been decided on if the invaders had managed to infiltrate their communications. As it was set now, Colonels Adams and Hoffman would position their B-25 and circle the NAF El Centro at 10,000 feet, acting as an aerial command center and reporting the status of the attack back to the March Command Center—with the B-17 bombers holding at 20,000 feet in case they were needed. When the ground troops attacked their targets, they would then break radio silence and contact the aerial command center on the B-25 American Pride. Target areas would then be marked with smoke grenades while the support fighters and the A-26 Invader strafed them. After the initial suppression by the ground support aircraft, the Rangers and Marines would make their drop over the airfield.

At 0712 hrs., a series of three beeps went out over the CB radio net broadcast from the American Pride. Ground forces at that time started taking out the enemy's forward observation posts and the two mobile radar units with small arms fire as they ran from outpost to outpost. After hearing the gunfire and explosions, the remainder of the ground forces began to stage their attack on the enemy forces and open an area for the paratroopers to land.

While running between the buildings, the ground troops launched hand grenades into various buildings—some they believed were used by enemy troops as barracks and storage for equipment. As enemy troops ran out of these areas, and in some cases toward them, the ground resistance forces provided suppressive fire. Then from the east and out of the sun came a wave of vintage fighters dropping low to the ground, raking the areas with 50-caliber rounds that caused small explosions when hitting some of the munitions storage structures. During all this, there were screams from enemy officers and alarm whistles being sounded as enemy soldiers ran toward the shooting from various areas of the installation. General Sheda came out from his headquarters building with two other officers shouting orders that the men were relaying to subordinates through portable radios. He shouted to another officer, "How do they do this? We neutralized their air forces!" Both Sheda and the officer dove off the steps of the headquarters building and behind a cement abutment as the steps were raked by machine gun fire from a strafing pass of a P-40 Warhawk. General Sheda then grabbed the portable radio from his assistant and called out to one of his Brigade Commanders, "I want you to put RPGs on those aircraft!" With that order, he could see some of his soldiers taking RPGs out of their vehicles and scanning the sky.

General Sheda then heard the drone of multiple aircraft engines and out of the east he could see three propeller-driven larger aircraft approaching the center of the airfield. The General caught the attention of one of his officers, who was standing with men holding several RPGs pointed at the approaching aircraft. As the aircraft closed in on center field, a line of parachutes could be seen leaving its back. The enemy officer pointed at the lead C-47 and yelled an order to one of his men holding an RPG. The soldier aimed into the sky and fired. The rocket, which is just a line of sight weapon, trailed a long stream of smoke as it shot into the air. It was just a lucky shot, but it hit just below the co-pilot's window on the lead C-47, enveloping the aircraft's cockpit in flames. The C-47 rolled sharply to the right and plummeted toward the ground, with its 15 Rangers still trapped in the back unable to get out of the plane. It exploded into a massive fireball as it hit the ground.

The remaining Rangers and recon Marines, along with the rest of the battalion from the other two planes, made it to the ground under heavy small arms fire with only a few casualties, while the A-26 Invader did a low-level strafing run between them and the enemy forces near the hangars. Quickly removing their harnesses, the Rangers immediately went on the offensive and pushed toward the enemy headquarters. FBI Special Agents James Hansen and Sue Grafton were embedded into the 3rd platoon, tasked with taking the headquarters building along with capturing General Sheda. The 1st Platoon took the area to the left of the headquarters building and the 2nd platoon took the area to the right. Their advance on the building was a pincer move between them and the resistance forces that had gone in earlier and led the path for the assault, while the other two platoons fought on each flank.

The squad that Agents Hansen and Grafton were assigned to made it behind a five-ton truck that was parked about 100 feet from the entrance to the headquarters building. Looking through his binoculars Agent Hansen saw a figure in a general's uniform barking orders. "Son of a bitch! That's Sheda! Right there!" Agent Hansen exclaimed to the Ranger Captain kneeling next to him behind the nose of the truck. "That's him. We have to capture that asshole, Captain!"

"Roger that!" replied the Captain, as he gave hand signals to his squad indicating the target and what they were going to do.

The Rangers of the 3rd platoon made their move and came out from behind the truck running in an arc toward Sheda, losing a couple men to return fire from Sheda's guards. General Sheda and one of his aides turned and started to run toward a Humvee that had pulled up about 50 feet from them. General Sheda and his aide made it within 30 feet of the Humvee when it exploded due to a well-placed shot from a U.S. Army M4 with an attached grenade launcher. The two enemy officers stopped and turned around, looking in multiple directions as if a magical door would open that they could run through, but the only thing facing them were 10 U.S. Army Rangers and two FBI agents with their weapons aimed on the pair. As if by instinct General Sheda's aide raised his sidearm as if to fire on the Rangers, but he was taken down by multiple shots from several Rangers. Agent Hansen yelled out, "Don't kill him we need him alive!" He then yelled out to General Sheda, "Don't move Sheda, it's over!"

General Sheda looked at him, cocked his head, and then laughed. "James, it has been a long time, my friend!"

Agent Hansen answered right back. "We are not friends Sheda, that was a long time ago. Now on the ground."

"I can't do that my friend," retorted Sheda, raising his sidearm then pointing it toward Agent Hansen's head. In what seemed like slow motion, Agent Hansen watched as Sheda was hit by multiple rounds fired by Agent Grafton, saving his life. General Sheda fell with a soft thump next to his aide, his pistol and satchel on the ground.

"Motherfucker!" Agent Hansen shouted as he ran up to where Sheda lay, kicking his sidearm away from him just like in training. "We really needed this asshole!" Agent Hansen said.

Agent Grafton then reached down to pick up Sheda's satchel, looked inside it and handed it to Agent Hansen, saying, "Jim, look at this." Opening the satchel, Agent Hansen found a satellite phone, maps, laptop, radio frequencies, contact information, and a timetable with targets of the invasions listed. Looking at the sergeant, Agent Hansen said, "Sue, you may have just saved this day."

On the eastern end of the base a group of vehicles, some 25 trucks laden with men and supplies broke through the resistance squad that had been holding it and headed out onto the 8 Freeway east toward Yuma. What had remained of the enemy force at NAF El Centro was trying to make its escape and hook up with others near the MCAS Yuma in Arizona, which the ISIS invaders had taken the day before. The command B-25 received a status update from the ground forces that the NAF had been retaken and they had obtained invaluable intel. They also advised that roughly 25 trucks had escaped heading east toward Yuma. Billy replied, "Roger that, and we will take care of that convoy, out."

Billy then got on the radio and called to the B-17s, "American Pride to the Heavys, over."

"Heavy Leader, over," replied one of the B-17s.

"Roger that, I have a target for you, over. East of El Centro a convoy of vehicles, all enemy, repeat no friendlies, copy?"

"Roger that. Heavy leader out," replied the lead B-17.

A short time later, multiple explosions occurred just east of El Centro, with some flames reaching hundreds of feet in the air. It was quite a view from the American Pride's vantage point. Billy keyed the microphone, "Little friends, check out the Heavy's target area and make sure it is clear." With that, the fighters made several passes over the area and it was finally declared secure with the final pass of the A-26 Invader. A ground commander advised Billy he was sending two vehicles they had captured to head over there and make sure the area was neutralized. Billy acknowledged that and advised the ground support aircraft that there were two vehicles of friendlies heading over to the area they had just hit.

Smoke was drifting once again across the El Centro air facility, but this time it was from the U.S. liberation from invading forces.

As the Rangers cleared building after building, picking up a few prisoners in their final sweep, you could hear an occasional explosion from a hand grenade or a single round being fired from an Army M-4 carbine. The time was now 0815 hrs. and the battle had ended with 20 Rangers and six Marines being lost, along with two pilots of the C-47 and some 25 more wounded in ground combat. FBI Agent Hansen picked up a CB handset and called the American Pride, advising Billy that General Sheda had been killed but he had valuable intel for command. The base was now secure, and they had about a dozen prisoners in custody. Navy Lieutenant Commander Wood, one of the survivors of the original attack on El Centro, would assume command of the reclaimed base and the Army Rangers and Marine recon personnel would remain and bolster his force of survivors and area civilian volunteers. They would secure that area and use the remaining insurgent vehicles that were operating to support the Marine Corps base at Yuma and search that area for any remaining roaming bands of insurgents. He also advised that the information from Sheda was of such importance that it needed to get to the command center immediately. Billy asked him if the runway was serviceable and if it was, he would land, pick him up, and then head back to March Field.

"Affirmative on that Colonel, it's all clear for you. There are some shell craters on either side, but if you stay in the middle you will be okay," Agent Hansen replied.

"Roger that, we will be on final in about five, out." Colonels Adams and Hoffman set down their B-25 on the runway at NAF El Centro and with the plane still running hot, picked up Agents Hansen and Grafton, who ran over to them. With the agents on board, the B-25 started to taxi for takeoff from the battle-damaged runway when there was the sound of automatic weapon fire to the right of the aircraft. In an instant, a mist of red blood spread across the inside of the right windshield and splattered on the right instrument panel.

Freddie screamed out in almost a shrill "Billy" and slumped over unconscious as he lost blood from wounds fired from an insurgent machine ripped into his right side.

Billy screamed out, "Freddie is hit. I need help here right now," as he applied full power to the B-25 and started racing down the runway, barely missing the shell holes on either side of him.

Agent Hansen looked at Agent Grafton and shouted over the engine noise, "Sue, get up there and help Billy."

Agent Grafton got up to the co-pilot's seat just as Stevo was pulling Freddie out of the seat into the area behind the cockpit. He looked at Agent Grafton and just nodded with his head for her to get into the co-pilot's seat. Agent Grafton climbed into the bloody seat, strapped into the bloodied harness and looked over toward Billy, who was pulling back on the yoke and lifting the B-25 into the air with a slight bank to the left. Looking at Agent Grafton, he pointed to his headset before raising the landing gear on the aircraft. Agent Grafton nodded yes and put on the headset.

"Agent, to do you know how to fly?" Billy asked her.

"Just a few lessons, Billy. I never soloed," Agent Hansen replied.

"That's okay, Sue," Billy said in a calming voice. "From time to time, just take the yoke if I need you to; I'll do the other stuff."

"Okay, Billy, will do," Agent Grafton answered.

"Steveo, how is Freddie?" Billy asked softly with a sick knot is his stomach.

"He is gone, Billy. Freddie is gone," Steveo answered with his voice breaking up.

"Okay, Stevo, we have to get home. Check the aircraft for any other damage from that last round of gunfire," Billy said with his emotions flowing over into his microphone while he held back his tears.

"Roger that, Billy," Steveo answered as he covered up Freddie's face with a flight jacket.

"I'm sorry, Billy," Agent Grafton said while looking over at Billy with tears in her eyes.

"I know, I know," Billy answered, then added. "Let's get home, Sue."

Billy then advised all aircraft that it was all clear to head back to March Field and informed the command center via the CERT radioman that they were bringing back valuable intelligence and one KIA.

Agent Hansen then positioned himself at the navigator's desk on the bomber as he started looking at the material in the satchel. Looking at the cache of intelligence, Agent Hansen just shook his head and wondered if it was the arrogance of General Sheda that he thought this material was totally safe in his satchel or just plain stupidity. Then looking at the land navigation maps, he realized all the circles on the map of Riverside County in the area where Deputy Butterfield was arrested were most likely drop areas for other insurgents to use to resupply arms, ammunition, and other materials they may need for the invasion. Looking at other areas of the map were several areas within the Riverside and Palm Springs areas with similar circles and notes written in Arabic. Agent Hansen then opened a map of Nevada. His eyes widened and he mouthed "Wow"! That map had similar black circles in the desert as the previous one, but a multiple red circle caught his eye. It was around Nellis Air Force Base in Las Vegas, and more disturbingly, a similarly circled military installation commonly referred to as Area 51. Sticking his head between the pilots, Agent Hansen for the first time called Colonel Adams by his first name only, saying, "Billy, let March know to try and have someone who can read Arabic there when we land. I found some bad stuff here man, really bad stuff. Tell General Killdare we have truly critical information."

Billy replied, "Okay, Jim, what did you find?"

"I'm not sure, not sure at all, but I think it involves more than this operation here," Agent Hansen answered, looking directly into Colonel Adams eyes and then turning to keep looking at the material.

Steveo climbed back up to the cockpit area and stuck his head in between Billy and Agent Grafton. "Billy, we don't look too bad, but we have some hydraulic fluid on the deck back there; otherwise, I didn't see anything else," he reported.

As the vintage B-25 approached March Air Reserve Base, Billy put over the radio, "No victory passes before landing, not now, out of memory of those we lost today."

The large white M on the mountain north of the base was glowing brightly to them as a welcoming beacon of returning home. As Billy was going over his landing checklist, he began to line up with the northern approach. The familiar sound of the landing gear locking into place was comforting. Again, as he always did, Stevo was looking around the sky for any other aircraft that might be out there or any other hazards.

"Sue, get on the radio and keep the command center informed of our arrival," Billy instructed her.

Agent Grafton started calling over the CB radio that they would be landing shortly and which runway they would be coming in on. The crew of the B-25 was exhausted, along with being saddened over Freddie's death. They were silently reflecting on all that had happened that day and over the last five days as well. In addition, they now wondered what they had uncovered and what that would mean for them all. Once again, as the sound of the wheels hitting the main runway screeched, belching smoke after touching down, the crew felt a sense of relief at being back home safe. The other aircraft of the strike force then joined in, banking and lowering their gear to land at March Air Reserve Base.

Waiting for the B-25 to shut down were General Killdare, Major Martinez and several intelligence officers, medical personnel, and the other FBI Special Agents from DART. Walking up to them, Colonels Adams saluted General Killdare. As he returned the salute, he said with a without a smile, "Congratulations to all of you on this operation and I am so very sorry on the loss of Colonel Hoffman. Now, what is this urgent information you have, Agent Hansen?"

"General Killdare," Hansen said, "this was with General Sheda, recovered by Agent Grafton. It appears to be a timetable for the attack, along with other prepositioned enemy cells in the country, and I believe their objectives, and God only knows what this writing is on the maps so the need for a linguist. But most urgent, I'm not sure why there are multiple circles in red around Fort Irwin, Nellis Air Force Base including Area 51 in Nevada, and numerous other military instillations, sir."

General Killdare looked at Major Martinez and said, "Major take that and break it all down ASAP. Now gentlemen, we also have good news. With Tony's help and his CERT unit, we have managed to create an emergency communications grid going all the way to D.C. We were able to advise other commands of what was going on here so they could act. Colonel Adams, we also told them about how you and Colonel Hoffman used of your B-25 and these other museum aircraft to launch a counterattack. Other locations across the county have started to do the same thing, but they are few and far between as we know for now. Agents Hansen and Grafton, we were able to tell the FBI Emergency Operations Center in Washington of the situation and your actions."

"Thank you, General," agent Hansen said. "If you can relay to them that I will have a preliminary report off to them shortly, we'll break down this new intelligence immediately. Agent Grafton can help Major Martinez; she's one of the best DART analysts and agents."

"Our CAM and Motor Pool mechanics have been doing wonders and managed to get several more vehicles operational again and repaired several generators today while you were on the assault," Major Martinez reported. "They managed to use new parts from supply to replace burnt out components from the EPW blast."

"Yes, the Major and the rest of the base personnel have been using unbelievable techniques to get some things working again," General Kildare added.

"That's good news, sir. We'll have our aircraft repaired and will be ready for the next mission against these bastards when that is determined," Billy replied with stern defiance.

"Yes, Colonel. This is now proven to be our best offense and defense on our way to fight back and defend this country until our other systems can come back online," General Killdare said. Then, looking at the two remaining members of the B-25 crew and the two FBI agents, he added, "You know, Colonel Adams, you and Agent Hansen are so much alike, but you do play well together when you must. At first I thought I was dealing with teen boys having a slight feud, but I'm proud of both of you."

Both Agent Hansen and Colonel Adams shrugged their shoulders after hearing that and smiled at one another. "Oh, by the way, Agent Hansen," General Killdare said. "FBI headquarters told me to tell you that you and your team are assigned to us from now on, so you boys will be working together quite often, and based on this new intelligence you recovered, Agent Hansen, it looks like it will be very soon."

Colonel Adams put his arm around Agent Hansen's shoulder, pulled him close and said, laughing, "See, General, we are like brothers now."

Agent Hansen just shook his head, mouthed "whatever" and laughed. Then looking at General Killdare, he said, "General, don't worry about us sir; we'll be just fine working together," ruffling Colonel Adams' hair to drive home the point.

With that, small discussions broke out on that day's mission. General Killdare, in a tired voice said, "If we had an Officers Club that was open, it would be drinks on me because I think we all need one today and a toast to Colonel Hoffman. But, regardless, with this new information we're going to have to wait for any type of victory celebration."

Continuing, General Killdare added, "We won this first battle, but I feel this will be a long campaign to get our country back to normal from this invasion. Now, get some food and rest. Intelligence will look at the data and we'll decide what our next move is.

"These military assets that are circled are of concern and will most likely be our next endeavor," he added as the group walked back to the command center building.

There was a noise behind them and they turned and stood at attention and all saluted as the medics from the base clinic carried the flag-covered body of Colonel Hoffman past them to a waiting Humvee.

EPILOGUE

The invasion of America and the decisive battle to take it back took only six days to unfold. The assault on the El Centro Naval Air Facility by the New Air Commandos formed around using vintage American warbirds showed the ingenuity of the American spirit to reach back into history and use it to preserve the future.

The materials gathered for the retaking of NAF El Centro provided the American military and civilian authorities with the names of sleeper agents, locations, and their objectives. It also listed the timetable of the invasion, which included numerous targets across the U.S. that, if completed, would have permanently disabled any type of recovery within America.

Although several targets across the country had been destroyed, many more were saved from ultimate destruction by the New Air Commandos under the command of Colonel Billy Adams and FBI Agent James Hansen.

The Civilian Emergency Response Team program provided an emergency communications system that, when fully implemented, allowed for a nationwide response to the invasion. It allowed order to be returned to communities and other American military installations and units to respond to the crisis.

Numerous other Air Force commands followed the example of the New Air Commandos under Colonel Adams and FBI Agent Hansen at March Air Reserve base, rearming other flying museums to combat enemy cells operating in their areas.

Within the following months, local and federal law enforcement, along with the military, made sweeps across the country, breaking up the various terrorist cells that had been operating in the shadows for nearly two decades. These sleeper agents had made their way into many different levels of the U.S. military and federal, state, and municipal emergency and government services. Several other successful military raids were conducted by Colonel Adams and Agent Hansen and the New Air Commandos, and they eventually become legends to many who heard of their exploits.

One major thing the planners of Haboob Wind failed to take into consideration was the amateur communications system used by civilian response teams, which breaks out in the event of an emergency and runs in conjunction with but also independently of modern municipal and other government systems. They also failed to realize the vast number of flying museums that are privately owned with in the U.S. that fly vintage military aircraft—independent of modern computerized flying systems. These aircraft are meticulously restored, and the pilots of these aircraft have become experts in the tactics used by the warriors who originally flew these legends.

The enemy also overlooked the American spirit and can-do attitude. The nation bonded together to repair and restore the infrastructure that was destroyed by the EPW detonations and sabotage. It took less than a year to repair the damage, with much being done in the first few months after the terrorists were defeated.

The invasion and its suppression also resulted in a change in future military strategy. Although technically advanced, smart planes, though useful, would no longer be the multi-use aircraft they were once thought to be. There was a return to the use of more military aviation assets that could be used without all the advanced computer systems. There was also increased research into the development of protective systems that would thwart the threat of EPWs.

These events also forced the country's leaders to not overlook and dismiss rogue states as they did with North Korea and Iran. For years, U.S. leaders had laughed off North Korea's ICBM tests as failures, when they had been successful and were terminated by the North Koreans when the data they needed had been gained. As with Iran, it gave a real-life lesson in the sleight of hand used for distraction in the development of an effective EPW system.

ACKNOWLEDGMENTS

This novel would not have been possible without my wife, Lidia. With her love and support through this, it became a reality; she put up with my long hours of writing and working with my editor till all hours of the night.

For my daughter, Susan, an aspiring author in her own right and my daughter, Kathy, another amazing woman.

For my amazing mother-in-law, Lillian, who helped take care of me when I was so ill.

For my good friend Steve Scheunemann, an accomplished author and motivational speaker who gave me some new thoughts and encouraged me to finish the book.

It also goes without saying that I owe so much to my first editor, Wendy, an amazing woman who helped me create this book; and to Adrienne Moch, who did her magic with her red pen and made me look good.

Finally, without a doubt, I could not have finished this book without the help of US4Warriors/Veterans Publishing and its commitment to help veterans in the pursuit of the arts.

Thank you all.

CPSIA information can be obtained
at www.ICGtesting.com
Printed in the USA
FFOW02n2357070618
47024987-49328FF